Molly smiled. "To our idiot exes."

"Without them, we wouldn't be here now," said Ethan.

"That's true," she murmured, looking at Ethan's lips.

Ethan felt his heart rate rise. All it would take was one tiny movement, one lean closer, and he could finally kiss her. Finally feel Molly's soft lips against his own again, after all these years of memories. He remembered that sweet hot-chocolate kiss. The one he'd relived a thousand times over the years. The one where she'd climbed on top of him and held him down. The first slow, deep kiss after all their quick and desperate ones. The one that felt like it meant something.

He leaned closer and her eyes drifted shut. He felt her warm breath across his lips and breathed in her scent. He should kiss her now. He should do it. But then she'd regret it. Then she'd remember that he had guardianship of three kids and that there were rhinos in Indonesia that needed her help. And he'd be left alone again. He backed away swiftly.

Dear Reader,

This is my second Harlequin Medical Romance novel, and I'm so excited that I was allowed to write one about vets! I adored writing this book so much. The combination of a feisty female pilot reuniting with a grumpily sexy Scottish vet was a joy to write.

Thank you so much for picking up this book. I hope you fall in love with Molly and Ethan like I did and their adventures in the beautiful skies over Scotland.

Love,

Zoey x

ONE-NIGHT REUNION WITH THE VET

ZOEY GOMEZ

MEDICAL ROMANCE

If you purchased this book without a cover you should be aware that this book is stolen property. It was reported as "unsold and destroyed" to the publisher, and neither the author nor the publisher has received any payment for this "stripped book."

ISBN-13: 978-1-335-99321-2

One-Night Reunion with the Vet

Copyright © 2025 by Zoey Gomez

All rights reserved. No part of this book may be used or reproduced in any manner whatsoever without written permission.

Without limiting the author's and publisher's exclusive rights, any unauthorized use of this publication to train generative artificial intelligence (AI) technologies is expressly prohibited.

This is a work of fiction. Names, characters, places and incidents are either the product of the author's imagination or are used fictitiously. Any resemblance to actual persons, living or dead, businesses, companies, events or locales is entirely coincidental.

For questions and comments about the quality of this book, please contact us at CustomerService@Harlequin.com.

TM and ® are trademarks of Harlequin Enterprises ULC.

 Harlequin Enterprises ULC
22 Adelaide St. West, 41st Floor
Toronto, Ontario M5H 4E3, Canada
www.Harlequin.com

Printed in U.S.A.

Zoey Gomez lives and writes in sunny Somerset. She saw *Romancing the Stone* at an impressionable age and has dreamed of being a romance writer ever since. She grew up near London, where she studied art and creative writing, and now she sells vintage books and writes novels. A good day is one where she speaks to no one but cats. You can follow @zoeygomezbooks on X and Instagram.

Books by Zoey Gomez

The Single Dad's Secret

Visit the Author Profile page at Harlequin.com.

This book is dedicated to Cindy, Silver, Charlie Brown,
Snoopy, Mouse, Plip, Plop, Coco & Garfield,
and Scruffy Cat. To all the pets I've had
and all the vets who looked after them!

CHAPTER ONE

MOLLY RADIOED AN update on her position to her destination, Killearn Veterinary Surgery, currently sitting a mile or so northeast of her plane. It was protocol to keep them informed of her progress.

The radio crackled to life. 'Dr Wilde! This is Jon. We spoke on the phone. Have you got eyes on the surgery's landing strip yet?'

Molly recognised Jon's voice and his soft Glaswegian accent. He was her new clinical director and had conducted her job interview via video call. Due to the clinic's remote location, there was no requirement to keep in touch with air-traffic control, so Jon had taken it upon himself to become her radio contact on the ground. Molly could monitor any other nearby aircraft easily from her cockpit's instrument panel, so radio contact on the ground wasn't necessary, but it would certainly be useful if there were any problems.

8   ONE-NIGHT REUNION WITH THE VET

'Good morning. I don't have eyes on it yet, no.' Molly peered into the distance. All she could see spread out beneath her plane was a green-and-brown patchwork of fields, with the grey-blue sea bracketing the land to the west.

'You'll be its maiden landing. I mowed it myself.'

Molly smiled. 'Thank you. It's very much appreciated.'

Being the very first flying vet in Scotland meant that her new veterinary practice had elected to transform their unused meadow into a landing strip and their huge barn into a hangar in the months before she was due to start.

'You're very welcome. It won't be as smooth a landing as you'd get at an airport, but it should be just fine.'

It probably wouldn't be the roughest landing she'd ever made. Especially when compared with her time in Africa when she'd had to dodge the occasional rhino, or with the landing strip that covered the entire length of a Pacific island, which would have deposited her straight into the sea if she hadn't managed to come to a stop in time.

'I'll let you concentrate. See you when you land.'

'Roger.' Molly clicked off the radio and adjusted her headphones. The locals were certainly friendly. And there was the landing strip. A long green field with a marked smooth strip right down the middle, leading to a wide-open-fronted barn that appeared to be just the right size for her plane. She breathed a sigh of relief as she began her descent. Her beloved plane should be nice and safe in there. She'd had her plane for two years now, and had been flying for four. It had been her lifelong dream to be a flying vet, and the fact that she was finally doing it never failed to give her a thrill of pure happiness. Molly had designed and painted the exterior herself, named it after her favourite author and washed and waxed it faithfully once a month. Maybe she was a little attached. But she'd sleep easier knowing it had a safe place to call home.

The runway ran parallel with the sea, about five hundred metres to the west. Which meant there would always be a lot of wind interfering with take-offs and landings, but it should be manageable. She caught sight of a beautiful sandy beach and a few scattered surfers on the waves as she glided down to earth. They really had done a great job in making the strip smooth, and after a little bump and a momentary rise up, she brought the plane down easily and taxied up the strip towards the hangar.

10 ONE-NIGHT REUNION WITH THE VET

As she crossed from the grass to the huge, flat expanse of tarmac in front of the hangar, she saw something she'd missed during the landing: two smiling people watching her. She turned off the engine, yanked off her headphones and gave them a quick wave as they beamed at her. They waved back enthusiastically and clapped as she undid her belt, the noise becoming louder as she popped open the door.

As they approached the plane, Molly quickly ran a hand through her hair, trying to straighten it out a little. She grabbed her bag then jumped down onto the tarmac and was immediately surrounded.

'Hi! That was so amazing! I'm Lara.' A long-limbed, beautiful young woman with an explosion of brown curls grabbed her hand and shook it with enthusiasm.

Molly smiled back, nonplussed. 'All I did was land a plane.'

'And it was epic.'

'Welcome, Molly. We spoke on the radio,' said a man a little older than Molly, with short hair and eyebrows so blond they were almost invisible.

'Lovely to meet you in person at last, Jon.' Jon shook Molly's hand warmly, then stepped back, smiling. 'Come on in. You can meet everyone properly after you've had a nice sit-down and a cup of tea.'

Molly's cheeks felt hot from all the attention, and she was grateful for a moment to gather herself as they all moved en masse towards a one-level brick building just behind the hangar.

'Thanks for everything you've done to get the place ready for my plane. It looks great.'

'It was a pleasure,' said Jon. 'As I've probably already told you, introducing a flying vet has been a pet project of mine for years. I'm just thrilled you're making it a reality.'

They climbed a small grassy incline up to the building, and Molly took her first look at the surgery she'd be working in from now on. It was a gorgeous old building, built with warm brown brick and covered in brightly flowered hanging baskets, with pots of marigolds lining the pathway. They entered through the back and walked past several consultation rooms before reaching the reception area, where big windows with yellow-painted frames threw light into a large, welcoming, high-ceilinged room. Two people sat on yellow plastic chairs, each with a pet basket sitting by their feet, and stared at Molly. She smiled and nodded at them as she passed, guessing it wasn't every day you saw a small plane land right outside your waiting room.

12   ONE-NIGHT REUNION WITH THE VET

'How many people do you have working here in total?' Molly asked once they reached the staff room. She was fairly sure she already knew that from the interview stage, but she was feeling too overwhelmed to recall.

'You're number five,' said Jon. 'You've met me and Lara. Ellen's with a patient right now, and number four is around here somewhere. I guess he decided not to come out to greet you, but don't mind him. It's nothing personal.'

That sort of made it sound like it *was* something personal, and Molly couldn't help feeling intrigued. Had she done something already to annoy this guy? She'd only been here five minutes. Lara thrust a mug of tea at Molly, and she took it gratefully. Flying was thirsty work. She'd been in the air for about two hours, flying into Scotland from London. The day before that, she'd flown the plane into London from France, so she was understandably exhausted.

'Would you like a tour now?' asked Jon. 'Or would you prefer to find your digs and have a quick orientation tomorrow?'

She was due to start her first shift tomorrow morning. But her curiosity about the fourth mystery vet had given her a second wind. 'Let's have the tour now.' She smiled brightly at Jon. She had all afternoon and evening to find the small house she'd rented, unpack what little she'd been able to fit into the back of her plane and get some rest in.

But her curiosity would have to wait a moment, as Jon took her to the hangar first. He seemed very excited about it, which endeared him to Molly. Anyone who loved planes like she did was all right by her. He held the door open and Molly stepped inside. It was a cavernous space. One entire wall of sliding doors was already open to the view outside. And what a view. The hangar looked out over sandy beaches stretching off into the distance, and the ocean glittering in the morning sun.

Jon led her on a detailed tour through the consultation rooms, the storeroom, the overnight ward, the staff room and finally came to the door of the last room in the building. He knocked, then showed her in and introduced the man inside.

Molly wasn't sure what she had been expecting, but she certainly hadn't anticipated being slapped in the face by a visceral memory of one of the most humiliating moments of her life.

Jon knocked at the same time as he opened the door, which annoyed Ethan from the get-go.

Why knock if you were just going to walk in anyway?

Jon had been especially upbeat over the past few weeks, ever since he'd found 'the perfect flying vet.' Providing care for all the animals that were currently out of their reach had been his dream for years. There were so many rural farms and pet owners in the surrounding countryside who couldn't get to a vet, and so many places the vets travelling by car couldn't reach in time to help with emergencies. Jon had originally set out to employ a new vet and a separate pilot to fly them around. However, the cost had stopped the plan in its tracks. But finding a vet with a pilot's licence? A gift sent from heaven if you believed Jon. It was sort of sweet how happy it had made him, but Ethan would rather eat his own arm than tell him that.

'Knock knock!' said Jon, and Ethan rolled his eyes before he turned around, pasting a welcoming smile on his face.

That smile wobbled as he saw the woman at Jon's side. He took a breath and stepped back to lean on the counter behind him. The messy blond curls were heart-stoppingly familiar.

Seeing her sent a thousand different emotions thundering through him. But underneath all of them, seeing her face reminded Ethan that she was the one person whom he'd been with on the very worst day of his life.

Surely, this woman couldn't be her. Last he heard she was off in Africa somewhere, never to return again to the dull shores of the UK. He shook himself figuratively. Clearly, the fact that he thought of her so often had tricked his mind into seeing her in front of him. This woman couldn't be Molly. She was too tanned, for a start. Molly had always been so pale, like porcelain, and she never had so many freckles. *And* she never looked at him like she'd seen a ghost. Ethan's heart stopped. All the sounds of the room flooded back in, and he realised he'd been staring at her, open-mouthed like a guppy for a good few seconds.

'Here he is!' said Jon. 'Molly, meet Ethan James.'

Maybe this woman also happened to be called Molly. Maybe it was just a coincidence. Ethan forced himself to reach out a hand and shake hers. Her hand felt warm and small in his. A jolt of electricity travelled up his arm as he shook it and nodded hello.

Her look of shock transformed into curiosity. 'We know each other, don't we?' she asked.

'No,' Ethan said firmly. 'That's not possible.'

She raised an eyebrow and for a moment, he

was sure he detected a brief flash of hurt before she schooled her features back to a polite smile. 'Well then, it's lovely to meet you.'

'Likewise.'

His heart raced as memories from his university days with a girl called Molly flashed before his eyes. Her hands in his hair, her breath on his neck. How peaceful she'd looked, fast asleep, wrapped up in bed sheets the last time he saw her. The more he looked at the stunning woman in front of him, the more he saw things he recognised. The way her eyes flashed green in the autumn sunlight streaming through the window. The distracted way she tucked her hair behind her ears with both hands at once as she spoke to Jon. The way she stood, weight on the balls of her feet, ready for anything, always poised and ready to go at any moment. Her comfortable, confident, easy manner, like she'd never felt self-conscious a moment in her life—that was just the same as it always had been. He smiled at all the little things he'd forgotten about. They hadn't interacted a lot, until that one night. But he'd always noticed her; he hadn't been able to take his eyes off her. Ethan had to accept it. This really was his Molly. A jolt of shame over what he'd done to her hit him so hard he almost had to sit down. He had never stopped feeling guilty for not keeping in touch.

Suddenly, they both turned and looked expectantly at him, but he had no idea what they might have just asked him.

'You can really fly a plane?' Ethan blurted out without thinking. He tried too late to keep the incredulous tone out of his words, and judging from her expression, he evidently didn't do a very good job of it.

She tilted her head and stared at him. 'Yeah, they let women do that now.'

'My apologies. That's not how that was meant to come out.'

'Please try not to upset my new star vet before she's even finished her first cup of tea,' said Jon. For once, Ethan was grateful for Jon trying to lighten the mood.

'So how long have you been flying?' asked Jon.

'I learned to fly in Australia, just after lockdown.'

'What?' asked Ethan.

'Yeah, I got bored.'

'Right, me, too,' Ethan replied. 'I made banana bread.'

Jon laughed and tried to cover it up with a cough. 'We're lucky to have you, Molly,' said

18   ONE-NIGHT REUNION WITH THE VET

Jon. 'I'm sure you'll find our little Scottish village a bit of a change from the last few years of your career, but I hope you'll enjoy working here. We're a close-knit community, and if you need help with anything at all, just ask any of us and we'll be glad to help.'

'Thanks, I'm definitely ready for a change of pace.'

'That it will be.' Jon tried to pull Ethan into the discussion, and Ethan realised he hadn't spoken for a little too long. 'Did you hear where she's spent the last few years?'

'I didn't.'

'Molly's been all over the globe doing wonderful things, working for Veterinarians Without Borders. Let me see if I can remember what you told me in your interview, Molly. You spent some time saving baby rhinos in Africa. Then you moved to rescuing chimpanzees in Mozambique. And your most recent project was…' Jon hesitated. 'I want to say vaccinating livestock in Vietnam?'

'In Laos. But nice recall! You know more about my career than I do.'

Jon laughed, while Ethan reeled at how much she'd achieved since he last saw her. Yeah, this was his Molly. Now he thought about it, solo piloting a plane was exactly the sort of thing he would have expected her to end up doing when they were back at university. She'd always been a little bit different. He wondered whether Molly would be happy, living in such an isolated place as this. Working here was about as far as possible from the exciting, adventurous life she'd been used to. Judging from her previous work, she must have chosen to specialise in exotic animals after they'd parted ways. So how had she ended up in Scotland? He couldn't believe she'd stick around for long.

Jon clapped his hands. 'So, now you've met all of us, even Ethan. The one and only. The oxymoron. The only vet in the world who hates pets.'

'I do not hate pets,' said Ethan wearily. He'd been through this argument a hundred times already.

'You have to admit you're not a fan of anything small, cute or fluffy.'

'They're just not my area of expertise. I trained with large animals.'

Jon turned to Molly conspiratorially. 'He hates cats and dogs.'

'For goodness' sake, I do not.'

'Well, that's handy, because Mrs Bandersway has brought in her Maine Coons to get their claws trimmed, so you can take her now in room three.'

Ethan squared his jaw, exhaled through his nose, glared at Jon and grabbed his thick protective gloves. 'You're doing them next time.'

Jon laughed delightedly. Then seemed to remember Molly was there. 'Oh, perhaps you'd like to shadow Ethan for this appointment. Get the lay of the land in preparation for your first morning tomorrow.'

'No problem.' Molly smiled and followed Ethan closely all the way to room three.

Why had he said, so confidently, that they didn't know each other? Yes, he hadn't been sure at first. But deep inside he'd known. And now he was stuck working with her in close quarters. This was going to be a nightmare.

CHAPTER TWO

MOLLY STOOD AND watched as Ethan worked his way through five of the most enormous Maine Coon cats she'd ever seen. Ethan's certainty that they didn't know each other had left her confused and a little hurt. At the time, she had schooled her face to hide the dozen emotions rushing through her. She hadn't wanted to make a fool of herself by contradicting Ethan and getting into an argument in front of her new boss. Maybe Ethan had similar reasons, not wanting to discuss personal matters in front of his boss. Or maybe he just didn't remember her. But she remembered him. Who could forget those beautiful dark eyes, or that gorgeous husky voice and Stirling accent?

The cats had come in for a nail trim, and Ethan blinked warily in response to their fierce growls. The cat he was holding writhed in his grasp, but Ethan looked determined to come out on top. The cat hissed at him and unsheathed huge claws that wouldn't have been out of place on a big cat in Africa, and Molly stepped in, thinking Ethan might appreciate some help.

He flashed her a look of annoyance. 'I don't need your expertise in exotic animals to handle a domestic cat.'

Molly ignored his grumpiness and stroked the cat he was currently gripping, tickling it under the chin and cooing over its beautiful long fur to distract it.

She couldn't pretend it wasn't satisfying seeing Ethan out of his comfort zone. She remembered the rather relaxed, confident stride he'd had about him as a veterinary student, and couldn't help but wonder if it was as much *her* as the cat who was putting him off. At least that would explain why he hadn't come out to greet her with the others. Perhaps he'd known somehow that she was coming and decided to hide in his consultation room instead? It wouldn't have been hard for him to hear the name of the new vet before she arrived. And there couldn't be all that many veterinary-trained Molly Wildes in the world. Would have been nice to have had some sort of warning herself before she walked in and saw his stupid face right in front of her again.

It had to have been at least nine years since

she'd last seen him, when they were both in their third year of a six-year veterinary degree at Cambridge. Ethan had filled out a little since then. He had always been beautiful, but back at uni his brown eyes and long, dark eyelashes had still given him the look of a baby deer. Now that he'd grown up, his face had transformed into a more lived-in, rugged jawline, one now covered attractively in short facial hair. He was wider and more muscular in all the right places. Broader shoulders, thick upper arms and a wide chest that she'd tried hard not to stare at. His hair was the only thing that hadn't changed, still thick and dark, the exact same colour as his deep brown eyes. And still silky-soft-looking, like it was asking for you to run your hands through it.

He'd done quite the number on her self-esteem. He was one of the very first people she'd ever slept with, after two years of crushing on him from afar. They'd shared a staircase in the halls of residence, but they'd never really been in the same circle of friends. When Molly hadn't been studying she'd hung out with the performing arts society, while he'd spent most of his time with the sporty lot. But after they'd slept together, he'd disappeared before she'd even woken up the next morning. And not just disappeared from her bed; he'd literally dropped out of university. He

24   ONE-NIGHT REUNION WITH THE VET

dropped out, moved away, took everything with him and was never heard from again.

But now he was here, and clearly a qualified vet, so he must have transferred to a different university and finished his training at some point. What on earth could have caused him to give up his spot at Cambridge? And whatever it was, why couldn't he have told her? Molly smoothly helped the newly trimmed cat back into its pet carrier and shut the door, then returned to the table to help Ethan with the others. The cats were purring now, completely the opposite from how they'd started the appointment, hissing and swiping at Ethan's hand.

Ethan looked up to find Molly watching him, and he smiled. All of a sudden she felt nineteen again.

'Thanks for distracting them,' he whispered.

She took a step closer, almost unconsciously, into Ethan's orbit.

'They seem calmer now,' he continued. 'Would you mind taking care of the next one for me? I can talk you through it if you need help.'

Molly tried not to be offended. She was pretty sure she could handle trimming some claws all by herself, but she guessed she was the new girl.

'Here, take these trimmers,' said Ethan. 'I have an old pair somewhere I can use.' Ethan passed Molly the small scissor trimmers, and their hands touched softly as she took them. She felt herself flush at the contact and was relieved she could turn away to pick up a cat and hide her reaction. After Ethan had rifled through a drawer, he pulled out an old pair that looked awkward to hold and even harder to use. Molly had to admit it was sweet of him not to hog the good pair.

Once the cat was relaxed it was a very quick job, and Molly scooped up all the trimmings and popped them into the bin that Ethan held out to her.

'Just in case you thought being a rural vet was all glamour,' Ethan murmured.

'Although it might not sound like it, I'm very used to run-of-the-mill cases, as well as the more exotic ones.'

'Well, that's lucky, because I'm not sure you'll find many rhinos in the local area,' Ethan said drily. 'I fear you might find us lacking in the kind of excitement you're used to.'

Molly glared at him, the effects of his smile forgotten, now that he was making fun of her. She couldn't let her guard down for a second without getting hurt again.

Of course, this guy couldn't wait to get away from her nine years ago, just like all her other relationships since, so she probably didn't have anything to worry about.

His voice was deeper now, but those eyes were exactly the same as the last time she'd seen him, all those years ago. Back then she couldn't help but wonder if she'd been so bad in bed that the mere prospect of having to see her again had sent him running for the hills. She'd been mortified. But she'd told herself she was better off at the time. She concentrated on forgetting that boy, graduating from Cambridge, landing a job straight out of training and travelling the world, living her dream.

So it was incredibly annoying that that very boy was now apparently a drop-dead gorgeous man who hadn't lost any of his infuriating charm, and was pretending not to remember her at all. Well, that was fine by her. She'd accepted this job in the smallest of small-town Scotland so she could avoid any possibility of romance altogether. She'd had quite enough of romantic partners. Especially Lucy the livestock specialist on the Laos project, who had dumped her three months ago and was already engaged to someone new. They'd been together longer than she'd ever been with anyone. She'd even thought marriage might be in the cards, and then Lucy had dumped her with absolutely no warning.

Lucy must have been planning to end things for a while, but Molly hadn't sensed anything wrong at all. It was enough to make her give up on relationships altogether. What was the point when she couldn't trust her instincts or sense that she was having problems? How could Molly ever relax in a relationship again, when even the people she trusted the most could leave at any moment with no warning? Molly took a deep breath and willed herself to think about something else. Yes, she'd been badly burnt, yet again, but this was her new start. One where she wouldn't be letting any gorgeous man or beautiful woman turn her head. Running into her first love could have put a spoke in the wheel of that plan. But if he was going to pretend he didn't even recognise her then that problem was solved.

Unless he wasn't pretending and he really didn't remember her at all. Unless the boy she'd never quite been able to get out of her head had lived the past nine years in blissful ignorance of her very existence. Maybe she was just that forgettable. She looked herself up and down in the reflection of the window. She hadn't changed *that* much.

There was a sudden commotion from outside the reception, and while Ethan finished off the

28 ONE-NIGHT REUNION WITH THE VET

last Maine Coon cat, Molly rushed out to see if she could help.

A man and a woman wearing jeans and gilets stood in the reception room, both wild-eyed and frantic, the man holding a large black Labrador in his arms.

'Please help her. She's impaled herself on a stick.'

Sure enough, as soon as Molly reached them she saw a thick piece of wood the size of a chair leg jutting out of the poor dog's belly. She reached out to help him bear the weight of the dog. 'Which exam room is free?' she asked Ethan, who had rushed out to join them.

'Room four?' Ethan asked the receptionist. After her quick nod, Ethan rushed down the wide corridor and held room four's door open for Molly and the couple. The dog safely on the table, Molly pulled a pair of gloves on. 'What's her name?'

'Hazel.'

'Hi, Hazel.' Molly stroked the Lab's head gently, checking her eyes and vitals.

'What happened to her?' Ethan asked the couple.

Still panting from exertion, and probably adrenaline, the man who'd carried her in spoke haltingly. 'She was running through the forest off-lead on our walk. She jumped over something and we heard a yelp. We found her just impaled on this branch.' He stroked the dog's leg and held her paw in his hand. 'Please help her. I'm sure she's insured for everything, but we'll pay whatever it costs. She's a member of the family. I sawed the branch off using my Swiss Army knife. Hope I did the right thing.'

'You did,' said Molly. 'That was quick thinking. If you hadn't, she might not have made it. She needs an ultrasound scan before we can remove the stick. Please make yourselves comfortable in the waiting room and we'll let you know the second we know what we're dealing with.'

Molly noticed Ethan raise his eyebrows and minutely shake his head at the floor. Was he annoyed because she'd taken the lead before officially starting her first shift? Well, tough. She had no time for office politics. The couple quickly gave Hazel a careful kiss and a pat, before reluctantly heading out to the waiting room. Ethan injected Hazel with a sedative, which took almost immediate effect, then he and Molly carefully hoisted Hazel onto a stretcher and wheeled her straight through a swing door that led to the ultrasound room.

After conducting the ultrasound, Ethan studied the image on the screen. They both stared at what was very obviously the pointed end of the stick lodged firmly in Hazel's liver.

'I'll go out and tell them Hazel needs immediate surgery,' said Molly.

Ethan nodded. 'Thanks. I'll get her ready.'

Once Molly rejoined Ethan, Hazel had already been manipulated onto her back. Her face lay to the side, and she remained completely unconscious. The stick jutted horribly up from her belly, and Ethan was just finishing up as he shaved off a large patch of fur around the wound. Hazel's poor belly showed up pale through her shaved black fur.

They both dressed in gowns and pulled on blue latex gloves, standing either side of Hazel, and got down to it. After twenty minutes of surgery, Molly could finally pull out the stick with a pair of pincers. She gently started to remove it, marvelling at how it just kept coming. Finally, it was all out, and she dropped it onto the waiting tray with a thump. Ethan checked inside the wound to make sure no splinters remained, then all that was left was to repair Hazel's damaged liver and torn diaphragm.

Molly assisted while Ethan operated. She watched his deft fingers working quickly and efficiently to repair the wound in the liver. It was impressive work, and as Molly watched

Ethan work on Hazel she resisted the temptation to confront him. How dare he not remember her? Or for that matter, lie and pretend not to. She wasn't sure which was worse. Was it better to be lied to or forgotten? If only she'd challenged Ethan immediately; perhaps if they'd been alone she would have. But this wasn't the time for confrontation. They had to concentrate on the patient. Molly used the suction pipe to remove blood from the area, to help Ethan see more clearly what he was doing.

'Excuse me.' Ethan reached past her to grab an instrument from the trolley, and Molly didn't lean out of the way in time. Thus, for five unbearable, exquisite seconds she was in close contact to Ethan's warm, firm body as he quickly picked up and dropped the scalpels until he found the one he wanted. She could feel his breath on her cheek and smell his aftershave. Something woodsy and delicious.

Hazel's blood pressure monitor alarm went off, making Molly jump. They both ran numerous checks, Molly's tension rising with every second, but when Ethan adjusted the intravenous fluids, Hazel's blood pressure level and heart rate finally returned to normal. Before Molly knew it, two hours had passed by in a flash. Ethan sewed his last stitch in the three-inch wound. Molly cleaned the area one last time with a sterile swab, and they were done. Molly blinked at Ethan, only now realising how close their heads had been this whole time—she'd been so focused on treating Hazel. Ethan wiped the sweat off his brow with his sleeve, and as he pulled off his gown and gloves and threw them in the bin, his hair was a tousled mess and his eyes looked bright and excited.

'That was amazing. Nice work.'

'You, too,' Molly managed to say, breathless all of a sudden.

'Do you think they'll want the stick?'

Molly laughed. 'Now we can be pretty sure Hazel will recover, yeah, it'll probably make a collectable talking point.'

Ethan looked at it. 'Jesus, it's huge. Let's measure it.' He grabbed a ruler from a shelf by the window and laid it next to the stick, then snapped a photo with his phone.

'They're not the only ones who keep weird collectables,' Molly mumbled, more to herself. The piece of stick measured twenty-one centimetres. Fifteen centimetres of which were still lightly stained red from poor Hazel's blood. Molly felt her cheeks flush as she remembered something. She'd kept her own memento of the night she and Ethan had spent together. Ethan had left his T-shirt behind, and even in the aftermath she hadn't been able to bring herself to throw it out. In the end she'd kept it, telling herself it would serve as a reminder to never be that vulnerable again.

While Hazel was taken for post-op care, Molly happily told the owners they were confident she'd eventually make a full recovery, and they would be closely monitoring Hazel for any signs of complications, such as infection. She went on to explain the aftercare instructions, medication details and follow-up visits. They were so relieved. Molly couldn't remember the last time she'd felt so fulfilled. She had spent the past few years in locations all over the world treating wild animals who had no owners. She'd loved it, but it did lack something. She'd known she wanted to get away from her usual life and find something completely different, but she hadn't known quite what she was looking for. Maybe this was part of it. Maybe the human interaction made more of a difference than she'd realised. She hadn't just saved a beautiful creature…she'd saved a beloved pet who was part of a family.

After they finished up with the black Labrador, Jon convinced Molly it was time to go home. Her first day was supposed to have been tomorrow, but she'd already done practically a half day's work. Jon promised she'd get paid for it, but regardless, she'd thoroughly enjoyed herself, especially after having helped Hazel and her owners. The new colleagues she'd met were so nice, they almost made up for Ethan. However gorgeous he may have become, she had to remember he was still an idiot. And a duplicitous, lying, grumpy idiot, at that.

Jon had offered her a quick lift home, and when he reminded her she had a small plane full of her belongings to transport, she gratefully accepted. As Molly waited for Jon outside, the reality of having to work with Ethan started to dawn on her. She'd been so excited to start her new job and her new life. But how could she do that when memories of her old life kept holding her back? She didn't like the memories of rejection that bubbled up when she was around Ethan, and she was going to have to be around him every day. Seeing him had thrown her right back to being twenty-one. All her friends had known about her long-time crush on Ethan. She'd tried to get his attention more than once, but he was always with some other girl. The blank look on his face when they'd been introduced today just brought back all the memories of when she'd felt utterly invisible to him at university. Which in turn brought back childhood memories of being ignored at home by her parents.

Molly had always had to fight to be noticed at home. She'd been a surprise baby, an only child to older, workaholic parents, and was left to her own devices a lot growing up. She'd always been invisible to someone, and she hated it. She'd been a quiet kid, and it was at university that she'd tried for the first time to break out of that mould. She'd tried to become more outgoing, more noticeable. Tried to be comfortable taking up more space. And she'd gotten pretty good at it! She was way more confident and outgoing now than she'd ever dreamed of being as a kid. At least on the outside.

So when Ethan had finally noticed her, and they'd had that one perfect night together, she thought it was the start of something real and genuine. When he vanished the next day without a word of explanation it had let her down badly, reinforcing all the old hurts from her childhood. She'd never had such a strong emotional connection with a person, combined with such sizzling chemistry, and she'd never been able to find it again. Ethan had been the first person she cared about to reject her, but he hadn't been the last. And she'd tried to avoid falling too hard for people ever since.

36   ONE-NIGHT REUNION WITH THE VET

The thing was none of the people she dated, male or female, had caught feelings for her, either. And they'd all left her in the end. This felt like proof that she was nothing special. So why bother looking for someone special? She preferred to reject people before they rejected her. She hid her insecurities with bluster and overconfidence. She'd had to accept she just wasn't loveable. And that was okay. Not everyone could be. Some people were the type to get proposed to umpteen times, and getting married was just a matter of choosing which prince to say yes to. Molly's best friend Julie was one of those people. She'd had proposals from four different boyfriends before she settled down. But not everyone was like Julie. Some people just weren't meant to find the one.

Molly's last partner had dumped her and gotten engaged to someone new within weeks. And two of her other exes were engaged now. She was never anyone's 'the one'. She was just the practice girlfriend, the 'she'll do for now' girlfriend. Not the girl anyone wanted to be with forever. Everyone she knew had started settling down, and sometimes she felt like a misfit. She'd never wanted kids, a mortgage, or a regular nine-to-five job. Her parents had been slaves to their large mortgage and busy jobs. They'd supplied her with plenty of money and possessions, but hadn't given her any of their time or affection.

That left her feeling ill equipped to be a parent herself, and unwilling to get caught in such a life of responsibilities and drudgery. She'd always vowed that was not for her.

But she'd never been very good at picking people who shared her ideals. They always seemed to end up wanting more from her than she was able to give. Anyway, it was obvious she wasn't what anyone was looking for. And so what? She'd never needed anyone. She'd always been better off alone.

She could feel herself getting angrier and angrier with Ethan. Not only had he abandoned her at university, now his infuriating presence was also causing her to obsess over whether he was pretending not to remember her or if he really didn't. But she was going to put a stop to it now. Molly made a vow to herself. She absolutely could not fall for this man again. She didn't have to talk to him. She would only see him at work, where she would be civil, do her job and avoid him as much as humanly possible. Outside work she could forget he existed and concentrate on how lucky she was to be living in this beautiful place.

Molly took a deep breath. She couldn't let

Ethan ruin her new beginning. She would focus on the job. She came here to be the best pilot and vet she could be, and to avoid getting hurt again by steering clear of romance. She thought she'd have an easier job of it, since she'd taken a position in the most remote place she could find. But she could still do this. At least she'd be away from Ethan when she was in the sky. She could deal with anything as long as she had the freedom she felt when she was in her plane, the one thing she could always rely on to be there for her.

'Ethan! A word.'

Late that afternoon, Ethan had almost made it out the door. He stepped back into reception, where he and Jon were now alone.

'I'd like you to partner with Molly for tomorrow.'

'Sorry?'

Jon paused. 'Clearly, judging from your work today on the black Lab, you work well together, so I'd like you to go with Molly tomorrow on her first job.'

'With her?' Ethan felt ambushed. 'In the plane?'

'How else do you plan on getting there?' asked Jon.

Ethan couldn't have been less keen to set foot on any kind of flying tin deathtrap. But since there were animals to treat, he guessed he didn't have much of a choice.

He'd been right before. This really was turning into a nightmare. Just when life was exactly how he wanted it—predictable, safe and uneventful—she had to burst back in.

He admired how smoothly she'd taken charge as soon as Hazel had come in, but he hadn't been able to stop himself from shaking his head in disbelief. Most people might need a few days to settle in to a new job and feel comfortable, but not Molly. Part of him almost felt a thrill at the thought of spending more time with her. She'd always seemed like the sort of person people gravitated towards. He'd felt so lucky the night they'd finally spoken. He already felt that familiar need creeping back in. The urge to be near her, to bask in her sunlight.

But the guilt he'd felt over the years whenever he thought of how he left things with her was a thousand times worse in her presence. She'd been so unlike anyone he'd ever been with before. So utterly free and unselfconscious. He remembered every moment they'd spent together. Her hair had smelled like vanilla and her mouth tasted like the hot chocolate they'd shared. He'd had a reason for walking away from the best night of his life, but it wasn't one he'd had the time to discuss with her. He was sure she'd soon forget him anyway. Was he really going to continue to pretend he didn't remember her? How could he possibly keep that up? It would come out eventually. The whole situation was mortifying.

As Ethan strode up his garden path and ran up the steps to his front door, he could already hear voices inside his house. He pushed open the door and the racket became louder.

'Can you keep it down? I could hear you halfway down the street,' Ethan said. A little exaggeration never hurt anybody.

'Kai took my shirt without asking and now it's all stretched out because of his stupid yeti shoulders.' Harry brandished a blue T-shirt in his fist and waved it at Ethan angrily from the top of the stairs.

Harry and Kai were fraternal twins, with the same light brown eyes and the same shaggy brown hair. But Kai had shot up six inches in height and his shoulders had considerably broadened some time last year. And Harry was still indignant about it, however many times Ethan told him they were only fourteen and he had plenty of time to catch up.

'Kai, stop stealing Harry's clothes. Harry, I'll

buy you a new T-shirt,' Ethan said firmly, hoping Harry would hear the finality in his voice and let it go. They were only ever home from school for a few minutes before Ethan got in from work, but they always, without fail, managed to get themselves into some kind of argument. He was lucky Jon was understanding about him working school hours, so he could be there for his siblings once they came home. 'Where is Maisie?' Ethan asked, changing the subject.

'Here.' Ethan saw an arm rise from the sofa, which faced away from him in the open-plan ground floor of Ethan's house. The large hallway was open to the kitchen to his left, a wide staircase in front of him and the living room to his right. They had two large sofas facing a fireplace, with a TV above it. Ethan smiled. He was never quite so happy or contented as when he knew all three kids were safely at home and accounted for.

Ethan clapped his hands together. 'All my favourite people in one place. Who's hungry?'

The twins both shouted in the affirmative.

'Can we get a puppy?' Maisie called from the sofa.

'Nope,' Ethan answered and headed for the kitchen. Maisie asked that question at least once a day. He wasn't sure if she somehow thought he might answer differently if she caught him off guard, or whether she thought she might wear him down if she asked enough times. But she was sorely mistaken either way. The animals stayed at work. If he ever gave in and started bringing them home, he knew it would never end. There was always a new animal at work that needed a home, whether it was a kitten, a dog, a hamster, or a calf. It was hard enough keeping on top of a full-time job and running a house with three kids in it—a house, by the way, that would probably need a new roof in the next few years, and probably wasn't big enough for all four of them in the first place, now that the kids all needed separate rooms and couldn't sleep in bunkbeds like they used to. He just couldn't face the stress of moving. Ethan knew his limits. If he added an animal menagerie to that roster, his house would be a complete pigsty within days, and he would never claw it back. The kids, as sweet as they were, would never keep up with feeding, cleaning and exercising a pet. It would all be down to him. And that didn't even touch the issue that he didn't want them to get emotionally attached to yet another thing that would just end up inevitably dying and hurting them. They'd already had enough loss to cope with for a lifetime. The wisest move was to just keep saying no, as much as twelve-year-old Maisie's sad eyes broke his heart.

Later, after he fed the kids, he cajoled them into helping him load the dishwasher. They then retreated to their rooms to finish their homework—which was mostly code, he knew, for playing video games and messaging their friends. Ethan felt he could finally relax. He filled a mug with scorching hot coffee and took it out to the front porch, his favourite part of the house. A raised wooden deck, level with the front door, ran across the entire front of the house, with wooden supports holding up a small slanted roof. He could sit outside with a hot drink, even when it was raining softly, and watch the world go by. It wasn't raining tonight—in fact, it was unseasonably warm. The streetlights had flickered on, despite the sky still bearing the soft yellow light of sunset. He sank onto the swing seat Maisie had begged him to get, leant back into the cushions and held his mug on his knee, waving away a moth with his free hand.

His mind still raced from having spent the day with Molly. He'd handled that badly. He should have just said yes when she asked if they knew each other. But after he'd said he didn't know her it was too late to admit he did, without sounding like an idiot. Ethan had to wonder: Had he just looked vaguely familiar to her? Or did she remember exactly who he was? And if so, why hadn't she challenged him? Perhaps she didn't want to rake over the past. Perhaps she didn't care at all.

Just as he shouldn't. Why was he wasting his evening second-guessing what she meant? He swallowed as he remembered the flash of hurt in her beautiful eyes when he'd denied knowing her. Her eyes weren't the only thing that was beautiful about her. He always thought his memories must have painted her as more perfect than she really was. No one could be that beautiful. But she was even more gorgeous now, if that was possible.

Speaking of Molly or, more precisely, Ethan's apparent new job role he didn't ask for, he fished his phone out of his pocket then typed 'how many people die in small plane crashes per year' into the search engine. He didn't particularly like flying in a jet, let alone the prospect of flying inside a tiny propeller plane.

Apparently, the global number of civil aviation deaths last year was only in the hundreds. Hmm…not as bad as he'd expected. He sipped his coffee and kept reading. According to one study, the odds of dying in a plane crash were one in eleven million, which was much lower than the odds of dying in a car. Still, he thought, it only took one. Ever since he'd lost his mother in a car accident, he'd found himself a lot more aware of the dangers around him. He was now more careful, responsible and risk-averse than he could ever have imagined he would be. He had the twins and Maisie to think about. The person he'd been at Cambridge would have hardly recognised him now. He'd never exactly been Casanova, but he'd probably dated more girls in one month at uni than he had in the past several years. He'd been a little more like Molly then. Up for anything, thrill seeking, open to adventure. But now he couldn't think of anything worse. Ever since he became guardian for the kids, life had been a whirlwind of responsibilities and hard work. With help from his extended family, and especially Aunty Anne, he'd managed to finish his vet training at Glasgow, just over an hour's drive away. It was years of early mornings and late nights, but he'd finally qualified.

He was about to search for information on how many people survived small plane crashes and tips on how best to do so, when he noticed a movement across the road. There was something moving outside the small, green-painted

46 ONE-NIGHT REUNION WITH THE VET

cottage opposite his house. He peered into the gloom curiously. The house had been empty and up for rent for at least a year and he'd wondered if it would ever find a tenant. It was a nice little house with a huge back garden and a couple of yellow blossom trees he'd always been quite envious of.

'Oh, you have got to be kidding me,' he whispered to himself as he realised whom he was looking at. Molly was walking back and forth between a car he now recognised as belonging to Jon, and the cottage's open front door. Her arms were full of boxes and bags. And there was Jon, carrying a suitcase from the car. Ethan was about to reluctantly stand up and go over to help when Molly slammed the boot of the car closed. Apparently, that was all she had. She must have flown some of her belongings over in the plane, and Jon was dropping them off here. To her new house. Right opposite Ethan's. Ethan let his back fall hard against the seat cushion, and he looked up at the now indigo sky. This was going to be awkward.

He wasn't trying to eavesdrop, but in the still evening air, he could hear every word of their conversation. He heard Jon ask if she needed any help indoors, and heard her thank him and tell him to get home. Then he watched as Jon pointed across the road at Ethan's house and waved at him enthusiastically. Ethan inwardly died, then saluted Jon and nodded at Molly, who just stared back at him. This was probably the first she'd heard that she'd be living opposite one of her colleagues.

Ethan knew he should go over there and welcome her to the street, but he couldn't seem to get his legs to work. Molly hesitated for what felt like a full minute, then appeared to come to some decision, rummaged inside one of the bin bags piled by her front door, then crossed the empty road, heading right towards Ethan. As she got closer, Ethan could see the expression on her face. It was not friendly. Ethan winced. He wasn't surprised after he'd declined to admit he knew her.

She came to a stop at the bottom of the wide steps leading up to his porch. Her hands were placed firmly on her hips. She stared up at him and snapped, 'Ethan James, do you remember me or not?' Her eyes flashed angrily, and two spots of colour flared on her cheeks. She was remarkable. He blinked. 'Of course I remember you,' he breathed.

That seemed to ruffle her determined facade and for a moment, she just looked confused.

'Well, good, because here's your T-shirt back.'

48   ONE-NIGHT REUNION WITH THE VET

Molly threw a crumpled wad of material into his lap, and he opened it up to find something weirdly familiar.

'I think I used to have one like this,' Ethan said slowly.

'Yes, you idiot. It's yours.'

It finally dawned on him what she meant. This was the Joan Jett T-shirt he'd been wearing that night, nearly a decade ago. He'd never realised what had happened to it. But he must have left it behind. Had Molly really kept it all these years? She'd been travelling the world but had still somehow kept hold of his T-shirt? Surely, this must mean something. Surely, he must mean something to her. He felt another painful wave of guilt. Was it possible that she'd thought of him all this time, just as he had her?

Molly glared at Ethan, waiting for a response. Ethan wondered if he also detected a flash of hurt. 'So, what happened? Was I so bad in bed that you had to disappear from public life? Did I insult you in my sleep? Did I give you groin strain?' Ethan nearly spat out his coffee. 'What possible reason could you have had to disappear like that?'

'You did not strain my... Look, why don't you come up here and sit down. We can talk. Would you like a drink?' It was time she knew everything, past time, really. Ethan would finally have to explain what had happened to him. It was almost a relief after all this time. He'd wondered about her over the years. Where she was, how she was, whether she was with anyone.

She sighed and climbed the steps. 'Fine. You have a very lovely house.' She sounded almost reluctant, but Ethan would take a somewhat reconciliatory compliment when he could get it.

'Thank you very much. Coffee?'

'No, I'm good. I'm planning on sleeping tonight, not staring at the ceiling, plotting Jon's demise for making us fly together.'

Jon must have told her he wanted Ethan to accompany her on the plane.

'I wouldn't say no to a whisky or something, though,' Molly added.

Ethan raised his eyebrows. 'You never used to drink whisky.'

'No, I was twenty, going on twenty-one last time we spoke. I was a half a shandy or a pink Bacardi Breezer kind of girl. Things change.'

She had a point. Once Molly was settled on the opposite end of his swing seat, Ethan dashed inside and grabbed a bottle of whisky and two small glasses from the drinks cupboard. He was grateful that the kids were still upstairs. He had

50   ONE-NIGHT REUNION WITH THE VET

a feeling Molly was going to ask him some questions he didn't need an audience for.

But just as he opened the door to join Molly, he heard three sets of feet thundering down the stairs. He let the door fall shut behind him, hoped they would stay indoors and poured Molly a drink.

She took the offered glass and peered over her shoulder, through the window into his house. She frowned. 'Ethan, I hate to tell you this, but there are three teenagers in your living room.'

Ethan looked across automatically, just in time to see Maisie throw a very well-aimed cushion at Kai's face. He turned back as he heard Harry shout with laughter and Kai groan in mock pain. Maisie shrieked in hysterical laughter and Ethan winced.

'Who are they? Do you look after kids in your spare time or something?'

'No, I don't.'

'An outreach group for troubled teens?'

'No. No, they live with me. Full-time.'

Her mouth was a perfect O. 'When did you have kids?' She screwed up her nose and her forehead crinkled. 'Wait. How old are they?'

'Maisie's twelve and the twins are fourteen.'

Molly tilted her head, and Ethan could see her quickly doing the maths in her head. He decided not to help her out and just waited for her next question.

'Whose kids are they?'

'It's a long story.'

'Well, let's go back to the start. Let's pretend we only just reconnected.' Molly settled back into her seat and took a delicate sip of whisky. 'So, what have you done since I last saw you, nine years ago, running away from me and disappearing into a tiny dot on the horizon?'

Ethan smiled. But he knew now he had no choice but to have the conversation. The one that made people give him the sympathetic face and pitying pat on the knee, before an awkward change of subject matter. He took a deep breath and jumped right in. 'Do you remember I got a phone call that night?'

'That night?' She used her fingers to make air quotes. Ethan nodded, trying not to smile.

'I think I do remember. You woke me up with your talking before you left the room. I thought it was a fake phone call to get away from me, because you regretted us sleeping together. Anyway, I fell back to sleep because you were gone for so long.'

'No, it was a real phone call.' He paused. 'That's how I found out that my mother had died.'

'What?'

'My mother and stepdad were killed in a car accident. I went back to my room, packed up my stuff and got the train home that night.'

'Jesus, Ethan. I'm so sorry. I had no idea at all.'

Ethan shrugged. 'You couldn't have known. I didn't tell anyone.'

'Still. God.'

'It's a long time ago now.'

'Why didn't you tell anyone?'

'I'm not sure. I guess because there was so much to do back home. It felt like home and school were two entirely different worlds. I didn't know how to combine them. I didn't stay in touch with any of the friends I made there.'

'I'm so sorry. I feel terrible. That must have been so difficult.'

Ethan thought he saw a flash of guilt in her eyes for just a second, and he wondered what she was thinking. Ethan shrugged sheepishly. 'You didn't really think I dropped out of Cambridge just because I slept with you?'

'It may have fleetingly crossed my mind. But no, my ego isn't that big! I did always wonder what made you leave, though.'

Ethan smiled. 'Well, it wasn't you. You weren't that bad.'

Molly gasped and slapped his biceps. Ethan laughed and dodged her. 'I'm kidding! Listen, I can't say I remember every little thing about that night,' Ethan lied. 'But from what I do remember, I had a wonderful time.'

'I'm sure you did.'

'How about you?' Ethan asked.

'It was acceptable.'

Ethan laughed softly and sipped his drink.

'So, the kids…?'

'Well, my real dad died when I was a kid, and the accident killed my mother and stepdad, so I had to come home because I didn't have a choice. I was needed here. Those kids are my little brothers and sister.'

'Oh, Ethan. You were suddenly all orphaned?' Molly looked stricken.

Ethan nodded and finished the last of his now-cold coffee. Then set it down next to his empty whisky glass.

'I didn't even know you had siblings. I guess we really didn't know each other all that well. So, it's just been you and them since you left uni?'

'I've had a lot of help along the way from extended family, especially while I finished my training, but yes.' Ethan paused. 'Have I actually apologised yet? If not, I'm sorry.'

'Oh, don't. I'm mortified that I made such a big deal of it.'

'Don't be. I should never have just left you wondering. Would it make you feel better to know that I've felt guilty this whole time? I never forgot you.'

Molly smiled teasingly. 'Never forgot me, huh?'

'Yeah, you're the kind of person that sticks in the mind.' Ethan smiled. 'I vaguely remember you standing on a table in the college bar declaring that you were very much against the idea of the patriarchy keeping you trapped in the cage of being dependent, barefoot and pregnant.'

Molly laughed delightedly. 'I was insufferable, wasn't I?'

'I think it's almost obligatory to be a little bit insufferable at twenty-one. I know I was.' Ethan paused. 'So do you still think that?'

'I've certainly grown out of thinking every woman with kids is somehow a victim of the patriarchy. But giving birth is definitely not on my to-do list.'

Ethan nodded.

'I mean, no offence to them.' Molly gestured inside Ethan's house. 'I'm sure they're lovely.'

'You clearly haven't met them. You want to?'

Her horrified face said it all. 'Oh, I have

zero experience with children. They probably wouldn't like me.'

He nodded. 'Fair enough.'

He was pretty sure that Molly was wrong about that. When the boys found out he'd been talking to an actual pilot, their heads would explode. But it reminded him of what he did know about Molly. He remembered their one night together in vivid detail, and he still remembered some of the things she'd said on the rare occasions they'd shared space. They hadn't been friends, but they'd hung out in a group sometimes. He'd had a crush on her, but couldn't be sure if she felt the same way, until that one amazing night when they'd bumped into each other alone, without all their friends around them, and finally managed to make a connection. But even at that age she'd been the sort of person who knew exactly what she wanted out of life. Adventure, excitement and definitely no responsibilities. That was what he'd loved about her. He couldn't predict what she might say or do next, and it looked like she hadn't changed at all. Which he admired in a way. To know yourself so well at such a young age was impressive. Ethan hadn't felt like he knew himself until well after university. Maybe not even now.

One thing was still the same, though—his

level of attraction to Molly was still through the roof; he still felt that same irresistible pull. But he had to resist it, because she was all wrong for him. Her risk-taking, fearless nature that had been so appealing in college was now the opposite of what he needed in his life.

Even if he was the luckiest man on earth, and this attraction were to go anywhere, she wasn't someone he could encourage the kids to get attached to. She'd spent her whole career moving from place to place looking for ever more exciting roles. He still suspected she'd get bored of their tiny village in Scotland soon enough. She wouldn't stay. And she'd made it pretty clear she wasn't into having kids. He couldn't do that to the twins and Maisie again. Love was not in the cards for Ethan. No one could want him when he had three ready-made kids in tow. He'd learned that first-hand when he let himself and his family get close to his ex, Carrie. They'd met when she brought in her mother's sick poodle. They'd shared a spark immediately and dated for months. Long enough that he'd felt safe introducing her to the kids, since he'd believed she'd be a permanent presence in their lives. But that was his mistake. She hadn't understood the reality of having three kids in the house. She'd grown up as an only child, and somehow seemed to be under the illusion that the kids would do as they were told, complete their homework quietly and then be tucked up in bed by eight, and that she and Ethan would have acres of privacy and time to themselves. Once she'd realised how things really worked, a frosty awkward distance set in between them before she finally left him, snapping that she didn't want to be landed with three older kids that weren't even hers. It had broken his little sister's heart and hardened Ethan's. He'd vowed never to put them through that again. His siblings had lost enough people. As irresistible as he might find wild-child Molly, he had to provide a stable life for his sister and brothers. They'd had it tough; now they needed security and predictability. He would just have to keep his distance from Molly.

He felt melancholy and just wanted this strange day to be over. But first, he had to make sure things were straight between them. They'd be working together for a while at least. 'I'm sorry I acted so strangely earlier today.'

'You mean when you pretended not to know who I was?'

'Yes. But to be fair, you didn't exactly challenge me on it. When you didn't say anything else, I wondered if perhaps you didn't want Jon to know how we knew each other. I was just fol-

58   ONE-NIGHT REUNION WITH THE VET

lowing your lead. Besides, I almost didn't believe it could really be you.'

'When did you know?'

Ethan laughed once. 'When you casually said you learned to fly a plane in Australia after lockdown. I thought yep, that's my Molly.'

Molly raised an eyebrow, and Ethan flushed as he realised what he'd said. 'Not my, I mean, that's...'

Molly smiled wryly. 'I know what you meant. Listen, thanks for the drink. I'd better get back.'

'Lots to unpack.'

'You said it.'

Molly headed back over the road to her new place, her head spinning. She hadn't even had a decent look around her new home yet, but she didn't care, because all she could think about was Ethan. He'd been just twenty-one years old when he'd found out his parents had suddenly passed away. He'd had to make the decision to drop out of university, forget all his plans, at least temporarily, and head home to raise a three-year-old and two five-year-olds by himself. She couldn't even imagine it. He must have been terrified that his siblings might get taken into the system if he didn't step up.

She was drenched with guilt that she'd spent

the past nine years resenting him for disappearing. In fact, she felt a little like disappearing herself right now. Her cheeks flushed hotly as she remembered shouting something about groin strain at him not twenty minutes previously. Mortifying. How was she going to face him tomorrow at work? Part of her was sad that Ethan hadn't felt he could share such a terrible thing with her at the time, that he hadn't felt they'd had a strong enough connection. It was heartbreaking that he hadn't had more help when he'd so badly needed it.

He was so sensible and responsible now. Back at uni he hadn't seemed like that at all. He was the star of the rowing squad. Everyone had thought he was by far the most gorgeous, desirable man at their college, and he'd never been without plenty of attention. Well, he still had those beautiful brown eyes, his kind manner and the strong jaw. She shook her head. That wasn't the point. She'd had a point a moment ago; what was it?

She carried her boxes and bags into the living room of her new home and stared at the rather pathetic collection of belongings. She was almost thirty and this was all she had to show for herself. It wasn't like she'd ever wanted kids, but Ethan's home, from what she could briefly see through the window, had looked so cosy and welcoming. She'd been living out of a suitcase for the past few years. Her whole adult life actually, now she came to think of it. She'd moved from her childhood home into university, then lived on the move ever since. Her ultra-conventional parents hated her unpredictable lifestyle and abhorred the fact that she refused to settle down. And she couldn't pretend that hadn't been at least a tiny part of the appeal. What they couldn't see was that she was terrified of turning into them. But she was shocked to find herself envious of Ethan's life. That wasn't what she wanted at all—all that responsibility and a boring scheduled life, each day always the same, always looking after other people, probably never having time to yourself. Never being able to just go somewhere on the spur of the moment, always having to plan everything down to the last detail. She'd never wanted that. For the past six years, the only responsibility Molly had had was to her job. She was free to go and do anything she wanted, whenever she wanted. But how often did she actually do that? She'd been drawn to the remoteness of this job. Drawn back to the UK, away from living abroad and working on temporary projects, and month-long stays in wherever had a free bed. She was also drawn towards places where she'd have the time and space to heal from her latest rejection. So this was an experiment, and it might go wrong. But maybe staying in one place for a while and having her own house might be nice. She looked around at the empty room and stared at the squares of slightly darker carpet where the last tenant's furniture had been. Getting a sofa would be a start. She suddenly had a thought and ran up the stairs. She found the main bedroom and pushed the door open, relieved beyond belief that Jon had been right and the house came with a bed. A pretty nice one, too. A king-size, with a simple oak four-poster frame. She threw herself onto the mattress, bouncing up and down a few times from the momentum, and giggled to herself. The bedroom curtains were drawn back, and when she got up to close them and switch some lights on, she realised she could see across the street right into Ethan's house.

His porch was empty now. Ethan was inside the living room with the kids, watching TV and chatting, one of the boys gesticulating wildly. Her gaze slid up the house. Across from her, on his first floor, she could see right into a bedroom, lit dimly by the light from his hallway streaming in through the open bedroom door. Maybe it was Ethan's bedroom? Molly yanked her curtains closed. The location of Ethan's bedroom was neither here nor there.

Get it together, Molly.

She hadn't come here for another temporary fling. Especially with Ethan, who was far too tempting for his own good, and who had three very good reasons of his own why he wouldn't be interested in starting up anything temporary with her. And temporary seemed to be all she was good for. Not to mention that she had never been great at connecting with children. She'd always been brought up with the idea that children were just a nuisance; at least that was what her parents had led her to believe.

CHAPTER THREE

THE NEXT MORNING Ethan met Molly outside the hangar with two steaming cups of coffee in his hands and his medical kit, full to bursting, in a messenger bag strapped across his chest.

She ran up, dropped her bags and unlocked the door to the hangar. 'Are you really thirsty or is one of them for me?'

Ethan held the second cup out and she took it gratefully.

'I didn't know how you liked it, so I had to guess,' said Ethan.

'As long as it's hot, I'm not fussed.'

Once inside, Molly pressed a button and the entire front wall of the hangar began to slide open horizontally, until all four leaves slid away to the far side.

Ethan had never paid much attention to the big barn at the back of the surgery's property, but now he was there he saw the fruits of Jon's labour. Jon had talked extensively about all his plans, so much so that Ethan had tuned him out after a while. But it was clear that Jon had made a lot of changes to transform the place into Molly's hangar. He'd had it insulated, redone the floor to take the weight of a plane and widened the doors on the front of the building. Plus, he'd cleared the whole place out so there was plenty of room for maintenance and repairs. As Ethan followed Molly inside, he admired the new security camera system that Jon had installed. Although he was pretty sure no one local would even know what to do with a plane if they did steal it.

Suddenly, Molly darted over to the edge of the open wall and reached out for something.

'What is it?' Ethan asked.

'There's a butterfly caught in a cobweb.'

Ethan stepped closer and saw it, its red-and-black wings fluttering uselessly as it tangled itself farther in the sticky web.

Molly gently pulled the web away from its wings and after a few moments, the butterfly was free. It fluttered around Molly's head then danced off and away into the trees. Ethan smiled. Molly might be tough on the outside, but she clearly had a soft heart and compassion for fragile, vulnerable creatures. He looked away and cleared his throat. She might be adorable, but he was not going to let that affect his determination to keep her at arm's length.

'You ready for your first flight?' Molly asked.

'Ready as I'll ever be.' Ethan ignored his life-long dislike of flying and the drop in his stomach as he contemplated going up in the tiny plane. Ever since he'd become his siblings' guardian, he'd often felt like he wasn't doing a good enough job, that he could never be as wonderful a parent as his mother was. He was never going to be a person who would do something risky or irresponsible like bungee jumping or skydiving, nothing that could risk his life and take someone else from the kids. So getting in this plane seemed like a bad idea.

'She's the most reliable small plane there is. Can fly through almost any weather at all. Gale-force wind, lightning storms, you name it!'

He'd prefer not to, thank you very much.

'Jon just filled me in on our first job,' Molly continued. 'And it's not a particularly happy one.'

Ethan's heart sank a little. 'Where are we going?'

'We're seeing a woman named Winnie. Apparently, she has a big piece of land up the coast.'

Ethan nodded. 'I know her. But only by reputation.'

66 ONE-NIGHT REUNION WITH THE VET

'She has an elderly horse who's been getting worse by the day. It's thirty-seven years old and lost a lot of weight over the last month. She thinks it might be time to give the horse a dignified end. I've got all the details on where we're going. Apparently, Jon will be near the radio all day.' Molly frowned. 'He said he wants constant updates.'

Ethan smiled at Molly's perturbed expression. 'He's pretty excited about the whole thing. I'm sure he'll calm down after the first day.'

Molly grabbed a clipboard from the wall and started walking around her small plane, checking items and ticking things off the chart. Ethan took his first close-up look at the plane he'd soon be ten thousand feet up in the sky in. He blew out a breath. The drama of the day before had successfully knocked out of his brain the fact he was going to have to fly today. He'd barely flown anywhere in the past decade, certainly not in something this small. It looked like it could be blown over by a small breeze.

'It's safe, Ethan.'

'I know.' Ethan tried to wipe whatever doubtful or suspicious expression must be apparent on his face as he looked at her plane.

It was a beautiful aircraft—a spotless and shining white paint job, the wheels painted in a glossy burgundy, which matched the propeller. He tried not to imagine how easy it would be for a goose or even a pigeon to bash into that propeller midflight and cause them to crash to the ground.

Molly started pushing the plane out of the hangar and on to the tarmac, which led to the runway. Ethan paused for a second, shocked that the plane could be moved so easily by one person, then managed to collect himself enough to run after the plane and help, by pushing it from the other side. Even though it was clear Molly didn't need any help, he stopped pushing when Molly did. The plane's call sign was painted in numbers and letters on its side, but also the name *Verne* in script.

'Planes have names? Like boats?'

'They can.'

'What does Verne mean? If that's not too much of a personal question.'

'I probably wouldn't paint it on the side of my pride and joy for all to see if it was private, Ethan.'

Fair point.

'It's the name of the author who wrote my favourite book. Do you read?'

Ethan shook his head.

'Well, maybe you should crack open a book sometime.'

'Oh, I'm sorry. I've been a bit busy the past few years, not gallivanting around the world on an extended gap year.' He winced as soon as he said it. But from Molly's hard stare it wasn't clear whether she had taken it as the, admittedly terrible, joke it was intended to be, or as a serious jab.

'Sorry, that was…'

'Hop in.' Molly didn't let him finish. She pulled open a squeaky door and jumped in easily. Ethan scratched the back of his head nervously and took a deep breath, before climbing up into the cockpit. With difficulty, he folded his six-foot frame into the passenger's seat. They slammed their doors shut in unison, he apparently a little too hard, judging from the look Molly gave him.

'Please treat my plane like the lady she is.'

Ethan rolled his eyes. 'My utmost apologies.'

Molly pulled on a headset, then passed Ethan one. 'I need one, too?' he asked, and she nodded. 'That's how we speak to each other.'

He was dismayed to find that there was a control yoke on his side as well as hers. The control panel was an impenetrable jumble of buttons and dials with a large square screen in the centre.

How could anyone know what all of these did? He could never learn if he had a million years.

'Okay, ready for your passenger briefing?' When Ethan nodded, Molly quickly explained exit procedures and emergency equipment and how to operate the safety belts. The speech was probably designed to be comforting but only made Ethan more nervous. 'Clear?'

'As crystal.'

Molly nodded. 'I just have to do some more checks before we take off.'

'By all means.' Ethan was happy to wait while she did all the checks she needed, to reduce the possibility of anything going wrong. The cockpit was comfy but cramped, and his shoulder touched Molly's—no matter how much he tried to lean away and give her room. She typed something on the touchscreen and a map appeared. She then tapped through several screens, one showing weather, another showing numbers, and clicked back to return to the map. The land showed up as bright green, separated by the familiar line of the coast, the ocean in bright blue.

Ethan was somewhat surprised to find that Molly started the plane with a simple ignition key. He didn't know what else he'd been expecting, but this whole process was a mystery to him. The engine hummed smoothly, and she let it run for a few minutes before heading onto the runway. She pulled the yoke forward and the one in front of Ethan came with it. He parted his knees to make room and realised his knee was now pressed into Molly's. He tried to ignore the tingle that ran through him at the contact and shook his head at his reaction. Why did she still make him feel like a teenager?

Molly released the brake and pushed in the throttle. Ethan gulped as he felt the plane gather speed as they bumped softly onto the grass runway and continued along its track. He grabbed tightly onto the arms of his seat. He resisted the urge to squeeze his eyes shut and breathed evenly. It would be fine. Molly was a qualified pilot with lots of experience. Flying was safer than driving. They would land safely at the other end, do what they had to do and return without issue. His brothers and sister would not lose another loved one, he would not lose his breakfast and everything would be fine.

'You doing okay there, champ?'

Ethan nodded.

'We'll be okay. I hardly ever crash.'

Ethan whipped around to face her, and she laughed delightedly. 'I'm sorry, I'm just kidding. I promise we'll be fine. You might even enjoy it. Try to relax.'

She gently pulled the steering column towards her, and seconds later they left the ground.

Ethan only had the headspace to acknowledge two feelings. The power of the adrenaline that rushed through him as they swooped into the huge blue sky, and how incredibly sexy Molly was at the controls of the plane.

Ethan's nausea faded away as they soared higher and higher, and he got distracted by how beautiful everything looked. He'd lived here all his life, aside from those years at university, and he knew every inch of the place inside out, but he'd certainly never seen it from this angle.

As they flew, Molly started pointing to various levers, dials and buttons and telling him what they did and how to use them.

'What are you telling me for?'

'What if I drop dead midflight?'

'Is that likely?'

'Anything could happen. You just need to remember the basics so you can help me in an emergency.'

Ethan shook his head in despair and tried to take in some of what Molly was explaining. He was never quite sure if she was serious or messing with him, but at least she was never boring.

They flew for a while in silence, Ethan marvelling at how far across the ocean he could see from up here. Soon, he started to sense the plane getting lower. 'Where are we going to land?'

'There's a long piece of flat farmland to the south of her farmhouse. I've been assured that it's smooth and unobstructed.'

'You're going to land in a field?'

'Of course. You think Winnie randomly has her own landing strip?'

He hadn't really had time to think about it. 'Without offending you at all, you are totally trained in landing, right?'

'Nah, this is my first time.'

He smiled tensely. Knowing she was joking, but also knowing this was going to be a difficult landing either way. He gripped the edge of his seat and stared out at the rapidly approaching ground.

'Hey,' she said quietly. 'I've flown planes for four years. I'm a professional pilot. I'm very good at what I do. We'll be just fine.'

Ethan nodded, and finally felt able to relax back into his seat.

'This is it, I think,' said Molly.

The farm was stunning, even from above. A huge, long stretch that looked like three fields joined together was obviously the improvised airstrip. A large L-shaped house and what looked like a converted barn formed the living area, and several ramshackle barns and stables surrounded it, with paddocks dotted around, marked out with white wooden fencing. Various cows, pigs, sheep and horses munched on grass and hay and ignored the plane above them. There were thick woods on three sides, and a large pond, or maybe a small lake sat at the bottom of a grassy hill in front of the house.

'Wow, it's beautiful,' said Ethan, in disbelief.

But Molly was all business. 'It looks smooth enough. That's good. Believe me, losing a wheel to a pothole, or having a propeller hit the ground on landing is no joke.'

Ethan stared over at Molly. 'Thanks for those images.'

She shrugged. 'I've had worse happen and I survived. It'll be fine.'

Ethan took in her relaxed stance at the controls and once again found her casual confidence and sheer competency hugely sexy. The landing was extremely bumpy, but a huge relief. Ethan had been somewhat distracted from the landing by the X-rated thoughts rushing through his mind about the pilot, but he was ecstatic to be back on the ground. Molly taxied to the end of the landing strip, then turned the plane around, ready for the journey back. The plane came to a complete stop, and Molly turned off the engine.

'So, you know this woman by reputation?'

'I've heard about her farm, but we've never met. She sometimes takes in the odd injured animal, or aged-out breeders who might otherwise be put down by the farmer, and keeps them comfortable. Gives them a happy life. I've seen Jon set things up between her and farmers locally when he hears about an animal she might take. She's pretty elderly herself, so she's never come all the way into the practice. Jon's driven out here a few times, though. Think he delivered a couple of Gloucester old spot pigs to her last year in person.'

'She doesn't run the place all by herself?'

'I think she might.'

'Oh, wow. I like her already.'

'That must be her now.' A woman approached the plane, smiling widely and holding a hand up in greeting.

She looked like one of those very capable, nononsense women who could just as easily skin a rabbit as bake a cake and not produce a sweat over either. Ethan wasn't in the habit of guessing how old women were, but he wouldn't be surprised if she was retirement age, despite how sprightly she seemed.

They jumped down from the plane and she greeted them both with warm handshakes.

'I'm Winnie. Thank you so much for coming out to see me. I'm ever so grateful.'

'No problem at all. It's our job. It's lovely to finally meet you. You're pretty famous back at the practice,' said Ethan.

Winnie laughed. 'I'd offer you tea, but if you don't mind I'd like you both to look at Heather first. Then I'll make you all the tea you want. Might even throw you in a biscuit.'

She joked, but Ethan could see the sadness in her eyes. 'We're here to do whatever you need us to.'

Winnie nodded despondently. 'I'll take you to meet Heather.'

They walked towards the stables that were situated right by the farmhouse.

'She's the best horse you could ever hope for. The sweetest temperament. Never got sick. We've had thirty-seven long years together. She wasn't a rescue. I had her since she was a foal.'

'I bet she's had an amazing life,' said Molly. 'I would love to have lived here for thirty-seven years.'

Heather was in her stall, by a full bag of hay, but not eating it. She looked very thin, tired and just about done with life. Her eyes lit up a little when Winnie got close and opened up the stable door.

76   ONE-NIGHT REUNION WITH THE VET

'She hasn't eaten anything of note for several days, and she's lost a lot of weight. I think it's time.'

Ethan and Molly gave the horse an examination. Ethan wanted to make sure there wasn't something else going on first. The patient could be suffering from mouth ulcers or a problem with her teeth that made eating too painful. But unfortunately, they were soon satisfied that it was simply old age and there was nothing more they could do. Ethan's eyes filled with compassion as he turned and spoke to Winnie. 'I think you're right. It's her time. We'll give her a very gentle send-off.'

'I've got everything ready over by the trees.' She nodded towards the edge of the forest. 'I feel so guilty.'

'You mustn't,' said Ethan. 'She's had a long, wonderful life thanks to you. It's the kindest thing to do now. You don't want her to suffer.'

Winnie led Heather out of her stable. The horse was quite wobbly and hesitant in her gait, and it was clear, even without their assistance, she probably wouldn't last much longer. Euthanasia really was the only good option at this point.

'Here it is.' Winnie stopped at the edge of the trees next to a huge hole in the ground with a sloped end leading down into it. It always felt a little morbid but when it came to euthanising a big animal like a horse or a cow, it was only logical to perform the procedure at the place where they would be buried. Some animals were simply too big and heavy to move afterwards.

'You dug this by yourself?' Ethan asked.

'It's the least I could do for my best friend. Took me three days, mind.'

'I'm not surprised. You've done a spectacular job. And what a peaceful place to be laid to rest.'

The sun dappled the grass through the trees, and bees buzzed lazily between the wildflowers. Ethan would honestly have been happy to spend the rest of eternity here himself, if he wouldn't miss his kid brothers and sister too much.

Ethan sedated the horse to keep her calm. And Winnie said her last goodbyes while Molly and Ethan stepped back to get the catheter ready. When Winnie looked up, wiped her face with the end of her scarf and nodded to them, Molly stepped forward and patted Heather's neck softly, before carefully inserting the catheter into a neck vein.

'I'll be essentially giving her an overdose of anaesthetic, so she won't feel a thing,' Molly said quietly.

Winnie led Heather down the slope into the

78 ONE-NIGHT REUNION WITH THE VET

hole, and once there, Molly got the needle ready. 'Once I press this, it'll be fast. I'll take her rope as soon as I've done it, and you'll need to step away, because she'll go right down.' Winnie nodded, gave Heather one last long kiss on the nose and stroked her head as she watched Molly administer the lethal injection. Then she passed Molly the rope and walked back up the slope she'd dug. Winnie turned away as Heather sat back on her hindquarters and lay down, and Ethan put his arm around her shoulders, patting her arm. 'She's okay. She's going now,' he murmured. It was a pretty graceful fall, and Ethan was relieved. An awkward fall could be an upsetting thing for an animal's owner to see, especially as the last image they would be left with.

Winnie wiped her nose with a tissue and turned back, and all three stood in silence for a moment as Heather went to sleep. Ethan checked that there was no heartbeat with his stethoscope and confirmed Heather's death. Molly wordlessly removed the rope and halter and handed them both to Winnie.

'Thank you so much.' She took a few deep breaths, then seemed to make a decision to let Heather go. 'How about we head inside for a cup of tea before you go.'

'We'd love to,' said Ethan. He caught an approving look on Molly's face, and he smiled briefly, relieved that she supported him on this. They hadn't agreed on much so far.

They all ended up having coffee in Winnie's large, cosy kitchen. Molly chose coffee to keep her alert for the flight back, and Winnie also decided she needed a little extra vim to get through the day after a terrible morning.

'Your farm is beautiful. And huge. Are you living here alone?'

'I am. I have a farmhand who comes in every day to do some of the tougher work. And my sister lives nearby. She visits a couple of times a week for a natter. But I live here alone. I always said I'd work the farm until my last days on Earth. But, to be honest, it's getting a bit much for me now.'

'Do you have any children?' Ethan asked. He caught Molly frowning at him, and he added quickly as an afterthought, 'If that's not too personal a question.'

'Two boys. Neither of them are interested in the farm. They both left for city jobs. They don't get the chance to come back very often.'

'Well, they're missing out on some truly excellent coffee,' said Ethan. 'And one of the most beautiful places I've ever been. I can't imagine what they're getting in the city that they couldn't get here.'

'Oh, nightlife and strip clubs, I'd reckon,' Winnie joked wryly, and Molly laughed in shock. Even Ethan cracked a smile.

Winnie excused herself for a moment, and Ethan wondered if it was possible for them to pop out and see Winnie more often. He downed his coffee and got Molly's attention. 'You feel like doing some digging?'

It only took a second for Molly to realise what he was suggesting, and she smiled and nodded. They jogged back to the grave together. Ethan grabbed the shovel from where he'd spotted it leaning against the fence and handed it to Molly, then went to the tool shed standing open nearby and searched for another one for himself. They quickly worked together to fill in the grave as much as possible. He couldn't bear to think of Winnie doing it all by herself.

He thought Winnie was going to start crying all over again when she eventually came to find them after about half an hour. 'Thank you so much, Doctors. I'm going to plant grass seed and more wildflowers over her to make a grave marker. She loved eating dandelions, so soon she's going to help some grow.'

* * *

Back at the plane, Ethan threw his medical bag in the back and hoped the heater would be quick to warm up his cold hands. Molly was strangely quiet. 'You okay?' Ethan asked.

'Of course.'

'That was pretty intense for your first day. Have you done a lot of things like that before?'

'It was pretty intense.' She paused and looked over at Ethan. 'You should try it with an elephant.'

Ethan laughed once, but wondered if Molly was always like this, showing no emotion after a rough job. She clearly had a big heart; maybe it was just how she needed to be to get through work. Rather than letting her brush him off, Ethan decided to try to gently coax more out of her. 'It was pretty sad today. Thirty-seven years is a long relationship. Longer than any of mine, now I come to think of it.' He hadn't even had the opportunity to know his own mother that long. It was strange to think Winnie and her horse had known each other longer.

'It was sad.' Molly hesitated and brushed something off the wing of the plane. 'I suppose I'm just not used to dealing with people that are so personally invested in their animals.'

Ethan almost held his breath. Molly was open-

82   ONE-NIGHT REUNION WITH THE VET

ing up and sharing her emotions with him for what felt like the first time, and he didn't want to do anything to stop her.

'I mean, everyone cared deeply about the projects I've worked on, but the animals weren't part of the family, and I guess I just don't know how to—'

'Hey!'

Ethan swung around, frustrated at the interruption, to find a man hailing them from the farmhouse next door to Winnie's property. They stopped and waited as the man ran over, the moment gone.

'You the vets?'

Molly nodded.

'Sorry to bother you. You wouldn't have a minute to take a quick look at one of my sheep?'

'Of course,' said Ethan. He introduced himself and grabbed his medical kit again as Molly and the man shook their hands. 'The name's Jack. Sad to hear about old Heather.'

Ethan wiped his hands on his trousers, still grimy from the dirt he'd just spent half an hour replacing. 'She's not in pain anymore.'

Jack nodded. And as they rounded the corner onto Jack's field, he gestured over to the paddock at a lone sheep with curved horns.

'Here's Bertha. She bashed her head on the

fence a few weeks ago, trying to get her head through to eat the grass on the other side. And since then her right horn seems to be growing back into the side of her head.'

Bertha was already standing, trapped inside a tiny pen in the corner of the paddock. And she was not happy to see Ethan. Her eyes wide, she tucked herself against the far side of the pen as he approached. He spoke to her gently, trying to calm her down. 'Hello, Bertha. Are you going to let me take a look at you?' Ethan slowly climbed over the fence into the pen with Bertha. 'I'm probably freaking her out because I smell unfamiliar,' he said to the farmer.

'I'll give you a hand.' Molly leaned over the fence and wrapped her arms around the sheep's body, holding her still so Ethan could take a look. Ethan firmly held Bertha's head, looking closely at the horn, stroking her nose with one hand. 'I think we're going to have to take the horn off. But it's a pretty simple operation. I can do it right now.'

Ethan looped a rope around Bertha's neck and nose to keep her head still, while Molly snipped off the longer fur around her horn with a tiny pair of scissors.

Ethan emptied a syringe of anaesthetic into Bertha's head, then used a wire tool, similar to

84 ONE-NIGHT REUNION WITH THE VET

a cheese wire, to remove the horn. It didn't take long, and the friction generated enough heat that blood loss was minimal and cauterising was unnecessary.

Molly then sprayed the area with a blue antiseptic spray, and they let the sheep free, Bertha bounding away happily.

Ethan presented the curved horn he'd removed to the farmer.

'I'll give that to my grandson. He'll love that.'

'Enjoy!'

As they walked back to the plane, Molly murmured, 'Anyone would think you agreed to help that sheep just to put off getting back in my plane.'

Ethan laughed. Once they were seated, Ethan finally got to warm his hands by the heater. 'You've officially saved your first Scottish animal. How do you feel?' he asked Molly.

'She wasn't my first. I saved a butterfly from a web.'

Ethan smiled. He'd forgotten all about that. He looked at his watch. It had been three hours since they'd left the hangar, and Ethan already felt like he'd done a twelve-hour shift. He stretched and yawned, his back clicking. 'How has sitting in a plane made me so exhausted?'

'I think that might be more a result of bury-ing an adult horse.'

Molly had a point. It wasn't every day you had to do that. But it was better than the thought of poor Winnie having to do it by herself. Ethan was so glad they'd been able to come over and help her. Maybe the whole flying vet thing wasn't such a bad idea after all. Ethan still felt frustrated that Molly hadn't fully opened up. They'd just been starting to get somewhere when Jack had turned up and interrupted them. But after that, she seemed to shut down again. He could only assume that Molly had seen and dealt with some very emotional things in Africa and her other travels, and this was just how she had learned to cope with things.

CHAPTER FOUR

THERE WERE NO more long-distance emergencies or visits on the schedule, so they headed back to base, where it was Molly's allocated afternoon to tackle the paperwork. But all she did was get frustrated with herself when her mind kept drifting back to Ethan. He was obviously trying to get to know her better. She'd tried so hard to remain professional at Winnie's, but perhaps she'd done too good a job and come across as uncaring. She'd seen the clear compassion in Ethan's eyes; he was so good at expressing sympathy and care. But she knew if she'd put herself fully in Winnie's shoes, she might have started crying and not stopped for a good, long time after losing such an old, devoted friend as Heather. She just couldn't seem to get the balance right.

'Molly? Ethan needs you in exam room two.'

Molly abandoned her paperwork and followed Jon out, rushing into room two immediately, ready to glove up.

Ethan, halfway through an operation on a rabbit, glanced over as she entered the room. 'I'm not going to be finished to get home in time for the kids,' he said.

Molly nodded sympathetically and eyed the rabbit laid out on the operating table. 'And you want me to finish up here?' She pushed her sleeves up in anticipation.

'That's okay, Molly. The owner specifically requested that I do the surgery, otherwise I'd swap with you, but thank you for offering. Actually, I was hoping that maybe you could…'

Molly frowned at him, wondering what on earth he was getting at. And why he looked nervous to actually put it into words. Until suddenly it hit her. He wanted her to go and check on his kids. Well, his siblings. She wasn't going to help him ask her; he could do it himself.

'Could I possibly ask you a huge favour?' he finally managed to force out.

'Maybe.'

'Could you just drop by and look in on my brothers and sister, since you're walking right past my house anyway when you head home? I'll speak to Jon about it, too, in case you're worried he'll say anything about you leaving a little earlier than usual.'

'I guess.'

88   ONE-NIGHT REUNION WITH THE VET

'And then could you maybe stay there for an hour or two until I get back?'

'What? What am I supposed to do with them?'

'All you have to do is be there. Make sure they don't set the house on fire.'

'Is that likely to happen?'

'It hasn't so far. But maybe that's because there's usually an adult in the house.'

'Can't someone else do it? I don't know how to talk to kids.'

'You talk to them like you would anyone else. I promise, it's not rocket science. I'm sure you're perfectly capable. They'll love you. Please, Molly, there's no one else I can ask. Everyone else is at work or away.'

Molly sighed.

'You won't turn into a pumpkin at the sight of a child, you know. And you don't have to change any nappies. They grew out of that at least a couple of months back.'

Even Ethan himself had never had to change a nappy. They'd been three and five when he took responsibility for them.

'God, fine. I'll do it just to stop you nagging.'

His face split into a smile that felt like the sun coming out.

'If it helps, think of yourself as more in a bouncer role than a babysitter.'

That did sound slightly less intimidating.

'I owe you one.'

'Yes, you do. A big one.'

His eyes narrowed as if he was worried about this coming back to bite him. But he was too relieved to complain.

Just as Molly was about to leave, Ethan spoke again. 'I'll make you dinner tonight, if you want to stay and eat with us. What's your favourite kind of pizza?'

'Pineapple,' Molly said, smiling at the disgusted face Ethan made. Molly paused. 'Are you asking me out on a dinner date?'

Ethan held her gaze. 'It's whatever you want it to be.'

Molly's face flushed pink. She was flustered at how easily he'd turned the tables on her.

'Okay, but that doesn't count as the favour you owe me.' She swung out of the room, trying to regain some of her dignity. 'Don't be too long! After all, there's no one watching me to make sure I don't burn the house down.'

Molly was already having second thoughts as she left work and checked on her plane one last time, before she headed home. The evenings were really starting to get chilly, so she pulled on her gloves and rubbed her hands together to warm them up.

She wasn't joking; she really didn't have much experience around kids. But she'd faced plenty of challenges before, and she wasn't going to let this one stop her.

She used the key Ethan had directed her to take from his bag at the office, and let herself into his house. It looked like the kids had only just gotten home.

'Oh, hi, what're you doing here?' The taller twin dropped his school bag on the hall floor and stared at her. She was pretty sure this one was Kai.

'Is Ethan okay?' asked Maisie, starting to look worried.

'Your brother's fine. He's still at work. There's a rabbit with abdominal problems who desperately needs his help. He sent me to tell you he's going to be late.'

'Oh, okay.' Maisie shrugged.

They all headed into the kitchen, and Molly decided she might as well follow them.

'Will the rabbit be okay?' asked Maisie.

'I'm sure she'll be fine,' Molly answered. She certainly hoped so anyway. 'Is it okay if I hang out with you for a bit?' She thought they might not take too kindly to being babysat, and she should couch it in a less annoying way. Suddenly, and for no apparent reason, she really wanted them to like her.

'What was your name again?' Harry asked.

'Molly. I work with your brother at the clinic.'

'Oh, you're the one who flies a plane!'

'That's me.'

'That's so cool!'

Molly tried not to preen but there was something about kids saying you were cool that just really hit the ego spot. 'It is pretty fun.'

'Dangerous, though.' Maisie pulled a packet of sweets from her coat pocket and offered Molly one.

She accepted with a smile. 'Not if you're a good pilot.'

'I guess. How do you fit, like, a cow in the plane?'

Maisie's brother laughed at her. 'They don't put the animals in the plane, dummy.'

Maisie threw a sweet wrapper at her brother, and Molly jumped in to defend her. 'Actually, I plan to rework some space in the body of the plane so that in future we could, if necessary, transport smaller animals back to the surgery in case they urgently need to be treated with equipment we can't fit in the plane.'

92   ONE-NIGHT REUNION WITH THE VET

Maisie made an 'I told you so' face at her brother and he laughed.

Maisie apparently had a lot more questions.

'What's it like being a pilot? Do you have a boyfriend?' She paused for a second. 'Or a girlfriend?'

Molly grinned. This kid was adorable. 'It's great. And no, I don't.'

'Ethan doesn't have a girlfriend.'

Molly nodded and wondered where Maisie was going with this.

'He hasn't had one for a long time.'

Molly knew she should change the subject. This was none of her business. But she couldn't help but be curious. And Maisie's description of Ethan sounded so different from the boy she remembered at university. He was so popular, and he always had a girl or two hanging around him, desperate to be his girlfriend. And from what Molly could remember, he seemed to date plenty of them. 'So what music do you like?'

Maisie thoroughly ignored Molly's attempt to change the subject. 'Carrie was the last one. She was nice for a while, but apparently we scared her off.'

'Maisie. Ethan doesn't like us saying that,' warned Kai.

Undeterred, Maisie continued. 'Ethan pretended that she left because of him. But I heard what she said. She didn't want to be stuck with us.'

Molly winced. 'That's awful. I'm sorry.'

'We really liked Carrie, when she left I felt bad.'

Poor kids. This Carrie person probably shouldn't have gotten involved with Ethan in the first place, if she wasn't happy to take on his kid siblings. This was exactly why Molly always made it clear from the start of any relationship what her boundaries were, so nobody got hurt. Although of course, despite her efforts, inevitably the person who seemed to get hurt the most was Molly.

'Do you play video games?' Harry asked.

'Sometimes.'

At that, Harry pulled gently on her sleeve and headed towards the living room. 'Do you want to play a racing game?'

'I happen to be amazing at racing games.'

'Excellent.'

Molly threw herself on the surprisingly squishy sofa and bounced a little, before Harry dropped a controller into her lap.

After playing three rounds of games driving around Paris at breakneck speed, Maisie somehow tricked Molly into explaining the rules of poker with a deck of cards. An hour had passed before Molly even thought to check her watch, and she was shocked to find she'd been there so long. It was surprising how easy she found it to connect to these kids. Maybe she was just seeing them as an extension of Ethan; maybe she would have liked them whatever happened. No, that didn't sound right. Maybe she was interested in them because they were interested in her? Whatever it was, it was unexpectedly rewarding.

Maisie had just whipped out a deck of cards, when the front door opened. And in poured what seemed like ten lively, chatting strangers, but was only four once Molly counted.

'Hi, all!'

'Aunty Anne!'

'Don't mind us. We're just here to drop off some supplies for the weekend and see if Ethan's made his lasagne yet.'

Maisie jumped up and ran to check inside the double fridge. 'No, it's not in here. He must have forgot.'

Molly floated at the edge of the crowd now in the kitchen. They were all obviously very used to spending time there and all were bustling about busily, taking off coats, pulling out stools and fussing over the kids.

'Hi.' Molly raised her hand in a wave. 'I'm Molly, from Ethan's work.'

The woman who seemed to be in charge of the group of visitors threw her a warm smile. 'Hello, dear. Call me Aunty Anne. Is Ethan here?'

There was no way Molly was calling a complete stranger Aunty anything. 'No, he's at work, but he's due back at any minute.'

Anne stopped bustling and sat down on a kitchen stool and looked at Molly properly. 'You're the girl who's moved in across the road. The one Ethan knew at university?'

Molly nodded, and Anne gripped her hands warmly. 'It's lovely to meet you. I've heard wonderful things.'

Molly doubted she'd heard anything at all, but it was nice of her to say. She felt a warm glow in her chest.

'He didn't mention a lasagne to you, did he?'

'He did not.'

'We're having a street party this weekend. You're invited of course. And that was going to be his contribution. Never mind. I can whip one up to freeze and cook on the day. You don't have to bring anything of course. You'll still be busy settling in. Probably haven't even got your kitchen set up yet, I bet! Is there anything we can help you with? Any furniture you need moving?'

Molly's head was spinning from all the questions and information Anne had been able to squeeze into one breath. She still hadn't built her sofa or kitchen table yet; the instructions said it was going to be a two-person job, but she'd been putting it off, telling herself she'd manage it somehow.

'I can tell there's something you need! Uncle Dan here can help. He's all muscle. And the boys.' She nodded towards the twins. 'What do you need?' she asked kindly.

'Well, I ordered this huge new sofa and a table. And I haven't been able to put them together yet. They're too big, really. I just got overexcited. I've never really had a whole house to myself before.' Molly forced herself to stop talking. This was unlike her; she never shared her problems with a stranger, but these people just seemed so kind and genuine.

Anne clapped her hands together. 'Wonderful. Let's do it now.'

'Shouldn't we wait for Ethan to get back?'

'Oh, you're right. He'll wonder where everyone is. Okay. We'll get started on the lasagne, then after dinner we'll get your furniture made up.' She turned a concerned look at Molly. 'How many days have you spent here without a sofa or a table?'

'Oh, not many. I honestly just got here. It's not a big deal.'

'Ethan said you're an adventurer.'

Molly bet he had. That dig Ethan had made about her being on a perpetual gap year flashed through her mind. She hated that he thought of her as some frivolous fun-seeker. She wasn't flaky, or irresponsible. She just valued her freedom.

Anne patted her arm. 'Even the most adventurous of us need a comfy sofa to come home to.'

When Ethan finally returned home, he looked surprised to see everybody there with Molly. Surprised and perhaps a little pleased as well, at the very least that she hadn't let them burn the house down, and, she hoped, perhaps even happy that she'd done a good job looking after his siblings.

'Where did you all spring from?' Ethan asked, pulling his coat off and greeting everyone.

Ethan deftly pulled Molly to the side for a moment away from the others. 'I'm so sorry you got inundated by everyone. You didn't have to stay after they got here. They could have watched the kids if you needed to get home.'

'Oh,' said Molly, suddenly deflated but not sure why. Suddenly, she was irritated with herself. She wasn't doing a very good job of keeping her distance from Ethan. She had to work harder to remember that she could never give him what he needed: a joint caregiver for the kids.

'But I'm glad you stayed. I promised you a meal, after all.' He smiled and lifted his bag aloft. 'I got pineapple for your pizza.'

Molly soon got wrapped up in eating pizza with his family, helping them make lasagne to freeze for the party, and then trekking them all over to her house, where they managed to make all her furniture in no time. With everyone there, chatting and laughing, her house felt like a home for the first time. Suddenly, being included as part of a large, welcoming family made her feel strangely happy, not suffocated or trapped at all. Maybe there were positives to being a part of something bigger? Maybe it depended on the people and the family in question. She hadn't exactly been blessed with a responsive, inclusive family in the past. Maybe being part of a family could be a good thing.

Ethan looked at her quizzically across the room, probably trying to work out what on earth she was doing, gazing into space and thinking so hard.

Back at Ethan's house, after his family had gone home and the kids had gone up to bed, Ethan suggested Molly stay for one last drink. And to his delight, she warily accepted. She'd looked a little spooked when he first came home but Ethan was glad to see her relax a little. Molly was so fascinating to him. She seemed so confident on the outside but showed intriguing, brief signs of vulnerability underneath. He wished he could learn more about what made her tick. Ethan grabbed a bottle of beer from the fridge and poured Molly a glass of wine, and they ended up on the sofa, cosy and warm by the fireplace.

'So, what did you get up to without me?' Ethan asked. 'The family spill all my secrets?'

Ethan was only joking—he didn't really have any secrets left to spill. But when Molly laughed and took a sip from her drink, Ethan could tell from her face that someone had said something to her, something that she didn't want to mention.

'Was there anything?'

'Well, Maisie did happen to mention something about an ex of yours.'

'Ah, the infamous Carrie.'

Molly nodded.

'What did Maisie say? Was she upset?'

Molly frowned. 'Oh, no. Not exactly. She did seem to think that she and the twins scared her off, though.'

Ethan sighed and took a long sip of his drink. He'd hoped that he'd convinced Maisie it was all his fault Carrie had left. But she was a smart kid; she could see right through him.

'I don't mean to speak out of turn,' said Molly. 'But honestly, this Carrie woman doesn't sound so great.'

'That's an understatement.'

'Yeah, I was holding back out of politeness.'

A flash of something crossed her face, an emotion Ethan wasn't quite sure he was interpreting correctly. Jealousy maybe? Could Molly be jealous of his past relationship with Carrie? The thought made him feel breathless and hopeful. Ethan laughed briefly. 'She wasn't all bad. She just wasn't ready for all the responsibilities I come with. I can't really blame her.' Ethan picked at the label on his beer.

'I can.'

Ethan looked up at Molly.

'You four come as a package. She had to know that from the start.'

Ethan smiled. He was touched that Molly could see it from his side, especially as he would have expected her to side with Carrie, about kids at least. Molly just kept on surprising him. She was such a mystery. Ethan suddenly wondered if he'd been asking the wrong question. Molly had made it clear that she didn't want to have kids of her own. But that was a whole different issue from whether she could see herself being with someone who already had kids.

Theoretically, someone who felt like that would in fact be the exact opposite of Carrie, who had wanted her own kids and not someone else's. Ethan didn't particularly have any plans to make babies. He had quite enough on his plate with the three kids he had. A woman who might one day learn to love his family, too—that was the sort of woman who would be perfect for him.

'You think you have it bad?' Molly asked with a wry smile. 'How many of your exes got engaged soon after they dumped you?'

Ethan pulled himself out of his own head and thought about it. 'Well, I don't know about Carrie. She could be by now. That's got to hurt, though. That's happened to you?'

'Three times.'

'Three?'

'Yep. I don't know why I'm telling you this. It doesn't make me look good.'

'Makes them look like idiots, to be honest.'

Molly smiled. 'To our idiot exes.' She held out her wine glass for a toast, and he shifted closer to her on the sofa so he could clink her glass gently with his beer.

'Without them we wouldn't be here now,' said Ethan.

'That's true,' she murmured, looking at Ethan's lips.

Ethan felt his heart rate rise. All it would take was one tiny movement, one lean closer, and he could finally kiss her. Finally feel Molly's soft lips against his own again, after all these years of memories. He remembered that sweet, hot-chocolate kiss. The one he'd relived a thousand times over the years. The one where she'd climbed on top of him and held him down. The first slow, deep kiss after all their quick and desperate ones. The one that felt like it meant something.

He leaned closer and her eyes drifted shut. He felt her warm breath across his lips and breathed in her scent. He should kiss her now. He should do it. But then she'd regret it. Then she'd remember that he had guardianship of three kids, and that there were rhinos in Indonesia that needed her help. And he'd be left alone again. He backed away swiftly. 'I'd better check on the kids.'

'Yes. It's time I got home, too.' Molly stood quickly and looked for a place to put her glass. She looked almost as flustered as Ethan felt. He'd never felt so sexually frustrated in his life, but he knew he'd done the right thing. But he was so close to disregarding all sense and logic and just kissing her anyway. Before he could make a move again, Molly abruptly left the house and shut the door behind her.

CHAPTER FIVE

THE NEXT MORNING Ethan glanced out his window to find the unexpected sight of the woman he'd dreamed about sharing a bed with all night leading a donkey up her front path and into her garden. He'd woken up even more sexually frustrated than he'd been the night before. She was slowly and quietly driving him up the wall.

The kids were still asleep, so he quickly got dressed and jogged over the road to investigate. He followed their route up the side of her house and found Molly tying the donkey's rope to a fencepost in the back garden. He'd hoped he might be able to act normally around her, but as soon as he saw her, all he wanted to do was pull her into his arms and kiss her. Nevertheless, the way last night had ended filled him with awkwardness. He was better off pretending it hadn't happened.

'Okay, how did you manage to acquire a donkey before eight o'clock in the morning?'

Molly looked up, flushing pink at the sight of him, and appearing somewhat guilty at being caught. 'Jon mentioned a farmer with a donkey yesterday. He'd been asking about putting it to sleep. But she's healthy enough. Just old, and the farm didn't really have a use for her anymore.'

'Is she from the Taylors' farm over by the church?' Ethan recognised her. He'd treated her a few times for abscesses. He suspected part of the reason Taylor wanted to offload the donkey might be because he was getting sick of paying for treatments.

Molly nodded. 'I stopped by, and Taylor said he originally got her to protect the llamas.' She stroked a hand over the donkey's back. 'But they don't have the herd anymore.'

Farmers often kept a donkey to protect other livestock, like llamas, sheep and goats. They were territorial creatures and could be quite fierce when they wanted to be. 'Did they sell the herd? I'm surprised they didn't sell the donkey along with them.'

'Yeah, the new owner wasn't interested.'

'Poor old girl.' Ethan stroked her ears and she tossed her head happily.

'You know she suffers from regular abscesses?'

Molly shrugged. 'I do now. She's a handsome beast, isn't she?'

106   ONE-NIGHT REUNION WITH THE VET

Ethan glanced around her garden. 'Where are you going to keep her?'

'Jon agreed to let me keep her at the clinic in the stables out back until I find her a new home. I'm going to walk her over there today.'

'Well, after you're done with that, are you busy this morning?'

'Not really, why?'

'It might not be your sort of thing, but I wondered if you might want to come with us to collect the pumpkins for the Halloween street party.'

Molly frowned, adorably confused. 'Pumpkins?'

'Yeah, it's mainly an Aunty Anne thing, but everyone joins in. They decorate the whole street with pumpkins. Arrange them on the steps, line the paths, light them up. They string up lots of lights, too. It actually looks pretty good.'

'You don't have to convince me, I'm totally in.'

Ethan laughed, relieved she still wanted to spend time with him after the previous evening's aborted almost-kiss.

Molly hadn't been sure at first. She didn't want to intrude on what sounded like a family tradition, and after their moment last night, when she'd been so sure he was about to kiss her, she felt a little awkward. But Ethan had seemed so keen for her to say yes that she'd agreed. And she was glad she had. The genuine smile she got from Ethan felt like a warm hug. A hug she kept feeling all day, from simply being included in their day. She hadn't realised how much she'd missed out on, not having a big family around her.

During all the years she'd worked abroad, she'd only spent the occasional weekend dropping by to visit her family between jobs. She was an only child, so her close family only consisted of her mum and dad. She'd always been envious of people who weren't only children, and had wondered wistfully what it would be like to have a big raucous, loud, busy family. For the first time in her life, she'd found a family just like that, and was feeling the urge to be a part of it. But her instincts were telling her it was too dangerous to make that leap. It might be fun at first, but she suspected she would soon feel overwhelmed. She just wouldn't know how to navigate it. She was much better off sticking to her job and dedicating her life to animals, seeing as love let her down so often, as well as her parents. She was scared of getting hurt again, and that part of her wanted to keep away from Ethan's

108 ONE-NIGHT REUNION WITH THE VET

family to protect herself. Unfortunately, that part of her was also sometimes too weak to say no.

There was a pumpkin field on the edge of town. All throughout October, the farmer let people come and buy pumpkins, and apparently kept a whole small field at one end for the James family street party pumpkins. They could purchase them for a great discount, but they had to go pick them and bring all of them back to the street themselves. So somewhere along the way, they'd turned it into a big fun event.

They all got dressed up warmly in scarves, hats and gloves, and drove to the pumpkin field in two or three cars. Sometimes they could fit in two, but with Molly plus the gaggle of friends the kids had brought this year, they needed another. Ethan offered to drive his Jeep, and Maisie and her friends climbed in the back. 'Come with us, Molly,' called Maisie from inside the car. Ethan made eye contact with Molly and pulled open the passenger-side door. He stared at her for a moment, then winked. And although Molly laughed it off, it made her stomach flip.

One of Ethan's cousins drove an all-terrain vehicle with a large trailer attached to the back for all the pumpkins to be piled into.

'How many pumpkins can we possibly need?' Molly asked.

'You would be surprised,' said Ethan.

The field was covered in clusters of pumpkins large and small, tiny and enormous, in orange, yellow, green, white, blue and every combination. Some with stripes, some with spots and lumps. Everyone set off, wandering around the field in twos and threes, collecting pumpkins in the wheelbarrows that were lined up by the entrance.

Molly and Ethan somehow ended up alone with a wheelbarrow. Molly could feel Ethan's gaze on her at times, when she was sure he thought she wasn't aware. They collected pumpkins as they worked their way around the field. Molly fell in love at first sight with a tiny blue pumpkin. She wasn't sure whether to pick it now or leave it to grow a bit bigger, so she left it where it was, and they continued up the hill towards the others. Their wheelbarrow had a loudly squeaking wheel, and it reminded Molly that she needed to remember to get some WD-40 on the door of her plane.

Molly watched Ethan's cousin as he jumped on the all-terrain vehicle and started the engine. He drove it up the hill to bring the trailer closer to the pile of pumpkins they'd all amassed, then parked it at the top of the hill and jumped out.

Everyone started piling up the pumpkins carefully in the trailer, filling it with what Molly was convinced would be too many pumpkins for anyone to ever use. It looked like there were at least a hundred in there. Molly piled her wheelbarrowful into the back corner of the trailer, filling the only gap left. Now the trailer was full, everyone wandered away to return their wheelbarrows. Molly suddenly remembered the tiny blue pumpkin. She decided she couldn't leave it behind after all, and she ran down the hill alone to grab it.

Once she'd found it, Molly noticed something move out of the corner of her eye. Then she turned and watched, frozen in horror, as the trailer started moving slowly backwards. Ethan's cousin must not have pulled the handbrake properly when he parked it. It was so heavy with all the hundreds of pounds of weight it now carried, that it started to gather speed as it headed alarmingly down the trail. Molly immediately shouted out in warning, but she'd gone so far down the hill that no one heard. The trailer was destined to collide with the hedge at the bottom of the hill, but not before it mowed down the person standing, blissfully unaware, in the road.

As the rest slowly turned their heads, Molly realised it was Maisie. She spotted Molly, and smiled and waved, not realising what was coming straight at her from behind. Without thinking, Molly dropped the pumpkin and sprinted towards Maisie. The girl's expression turned to shock as Molly collided with her and pushed her out of the way, seconds before the trailer raced past them. Molly tried to roll underneath her so that Maisie would have a softer landing. She thought about how it had almost hit Maisie squarely in the back. And only once they came to a stop on the muddy grass did Molly realise the trailer must have clipped her, as her leg hurt like hell.

'Maisie, are you okay?'

The others ran towards them, shouting, and Molly sat up just in time to see Ethan rather heroically jump on to the vehicle and slam on the brakes. The trailer stopped just before the hedge, and not even one pumpkin rolled out of the trailer.

Ethan was at their sides immediately and after helping Maisie up, who thankfully seemed fine, he knelt down beside Molly.

'Where are you hurt?'

'My lower right leg.'

He gently took her leg in his hands and moved

his fingers up and down her jeans. 'There's no blood.' Luckily, they weren't tight jeans, and he easily pushed up the denim to her knee to take a look. 'No broken skin.' There was a huge red mark over one side of her leg. He touched one finger to it lightly as she wiggled her toes experimentally. 'That's going to be a killer bruise.'

'It doesn't seem to be swelling. Do you want to try to stand on it?'

Molly nodded, and he took her cold hands in his big warm ones, and gently, slowly, pulled her up. He kept his hands around her waist and encouraged her to put a little weight on her foot. It was sore, but it clearly wasn't broken. 'Oh, thank God. I think it's all right.'

He pulled her into a hug. Molly felt tingles everywhere their bodies touched. Almost in shock, she wrapped her arms around his wide shoulders and pulled him closer, his body warm against hers.

'Thank you so much,' Ethan whispered into Molly's ear, his words hot on her neck.

He pulled back slightly to look her in the eye. 'You saved Maisie. None of us even realised what was happening until it was too late.'

'Is she all right?' Molly asked. 'I took her down pretty hard.'

Ethan stopped hugging her so they could

turn towards Maisie, and Molly almost wished she hadn't asked. She was cold without Ethan's strong arms around her. But she was relieved to find Maisie all in one piece and smiling.

'You saved my life!'

Molly shook her head. 'Let's not go that far.'

Ethan took Molly's shoulders and spoke quietly, while everyone fussed over Maisie. 'I know I go over the top sometimes about keeping them safe. But that was real. She could have been knocked down and crushed underneath the trailer's wheels.' He shut his eyes for a second as if to block out the image. 'She would have been seriously injured. We'd be calling out an ambulance or a damn rescue helicopter right now. Thank you, Molly. I mean it. I felt like time stood still when I saw that trailer about to hit her. I'd be devastated to lose Maisie. I've lost enough already.' Ethan pulled back and stared into Molly's eyes, brushing a strand of hair softly out of her face and tucking it behind her ear. 'That was the most terrifying moment of my life. Thank you so much. I don't know how I'm ever going to repay you.'

And then Molly got another one of those delicious, bone-crushing hugs, and all she could do was mumble, 'No problem,' into Ethan's chest.

It hadn't really been all that dramatic, had it?

She only did what anyone else would have done. She just happened to be the only one who looked over and saw it coming. She didn't even get hurt too badly. Sure, she was limping a little, but nothing serious.

Even if she'd broken her leg, it would probably have been worth it to see Maisie safe. Both her legs. Maybe even more. That idea stopped her in her tracks. She ran the thought through her head for a moment. This must be what it felt like to have siblings, instinctively putting their safety before your own. Had she ever thought that about anyone like this before? She ran through a list of her exes. She wouldn't even risk breaking a nail for any of that sorry crew now. But at the time she was with them? No, maybe not even then. It came as a shock to Molly that in such a short time of being around Ethan again, and knowing his family, that she had developed such an attachment to them all.

She loved the way Ethan interacted with his family. He was their rock and the one person they all revolved around, the centre of their world. And it was making *her* long to be at the centre of Ethan's world. She felt like she didn't even know herself anymore. In fact, it was terrifying, and it made her want to run for the hills.

But she was soon invited out for dinner that

night. Molly was toasted at least ten times by various members of the family, and she had a wonderful time. Cosy, safe and appreciated inside the bubble of the James family. Despite that, there was a thread of unease pulling at her all night. Telling her that she wasn't really part of this family, that she'd never really felt part of any family, even her own. That she had been independent for so long that she was probably just enjoying the novelty.

Near the end of the night, it all got a bit too much for her. She excused herself and went out the back door for a breath of fresh air. She was only out there a moment, admiring the clouds her breath made in the cold air, before Ethan joined her.

'I just wanted to say thank you again.'

Molly sighed quietly. She appreciated it, but she'd had enough thank-yous to last a lifetime. 'I'd have done it for anyone.'

The hurt look she detected on Ethan's face before she followed him back inside made her regret her wording, but not her sentiment. She had to regain some distance.

Just after Molly got home, her phone rang and she glanced at the caller ID, expecting to see an unknown number that she would assume was an insurance scam and decline. There were only two people she answered calls from—her mother and her best friend. Molly laughed out loud when she saw Julie's name and the picture of her from first year that she still used for Julie's contact photo. She answered immediately.

'You haven't called me for ages, you miscreant.'

'Lovely to speak to you, too,' said Julie.

'I actually have missed you,' said Molly as an unfamiliar rush of homesickness ran through her at the sound of her oldest friend's voice. She sat down on the end of her bed, relieved to take the weight off her sore leg.

'Aw, likewise. And where in the world might you be today?' Julie teased.

'You know perfectly well I'm in Scotland. You liked my Instagram pictures of the new house. And the donkey.'

Julie snorted a laugh. 'I did. She's adorable. How's Scotland?'

'Cold. And beautiful. I actually feel really good here.'

'Oh, really? You think you might actually stick around, then?'

Julie sounded shocked, and Molly couldn't really blame her. She hadn't spent longer than six months in one place since she'd graduated.

'It's far too soon to tell. But you never know.'

'That's amazing, Molly.'

'And you will never believe who I ran into.' Molly's heart rate sped up as she realised Julie was the one person who would actually understand the magnitude. 'Well, I say ran into... I'm literally working with him every day.'

'Who?'

'Ethan James.'

There was a short silence on the other end of the line. 'The boy that slept with you and then pulled a total Mary Celeste on you?'

Molly had forgotten that was how Julie would remember him. 'Well, yes. But now he's explained why, and believe me it's totally understandable.'

'I'll have to take your word for that.'

'Honestly. It wouldn't feel right telling you the personal details, but I promise you wouldn't blame him, either.'

'Okay, I believe you.' Julie paused. 'So now we know why you're so open to staying!' Molly could hear the smile in her friend's voice.

The evening had turned a little darker while she'd been talking on the phone, and all the windows were lit up in Ethan's house. She really needed to teach him to draw his curtains.

'So what's he like now? Still a ladies' man?' Julie asked.

'Oh, my God, no. He's completely different from how he was at uni. Well, from how he seemed at uni. I mean, we never really knew him, did we? I'm not so sure he ever really was a ladies' man. I think we just believed the gossip.'

'I suppose so. But he had enough of a reputation that it seemed like we knew every last bloody thing about him, whether we wanted to or not.'

Julie was right. Everyone at uni knew Ethan James. The most handsome eligible man in school. The golden boy, with the pretty face and the come-to-bed eyes. He was rumoured to have slept with half the girls on campus, but Molly never knew if that was true or spread by jealous fellow students.

The night they'd spent together nine years ago had begun sometime after midnight at the tail end of a May Week ball. Somehow, Ethan had lost track of all his friends, and on her way home after a couple of drinks, Molly had discovered him sitting alone on the wet grass under a tree, looking dejected. She'd planned to walk past in elegant silence and say nothing, but she'd tripped on the edge of the path. He'd laughed, then tried to cover it up with a cough, and asked if she was okay.

She'd pointed at the grass next to him and asked, 'Is that seat taken?'

He'd laughed again and looked up at her with those dark, pretty eyes and said, 'Be my guest.'

They'd talked for hours. There was something about the fact that they were both sitting in the dark, and were finally alone together instead of being surrounded by their very disparate friend groups, which allowed them to finally click. He gave her one of his purple woollen gloves to help keep her hands warm, and they ended up going to her room to make some hot chocolate. She'd sobered up by the time she asked him to stay the night, but she was still running on adrenaline when he said yes. The night they spent together had been wonderful. Perfect, in fact. The odd previous fling had been nothing to write home about, awkward, stilted and utterly forgettable. But for some reason, with Ethan, it was everything she'd ever fantasised about from a romantic encounter. He'd even wanted to cuddle afterwards. Another first. And it was just as she was falling asleep, warm and safe in his arms, wondering what aftershave he wore because he smelled delicious, she'd heard him get a phone call. He'd whispered something, then shoved on his boots, left his Joan Jett T-shirt. And she'd never seen him again.

* * *

'You never forgot about him, did you?' asked Julie.

Molly almost denied it, but decided at the last minute she was sick of pretending. 'Not for want of trying.'

'Are you sure you didn't know he would be there?'

'Yes, it was a total shock. Apparently, this is the village he was born in, and I guess he's never really wanted to leave.'

'Hmm.' Julie hummed thoughtfully. 'You did sleep with him. And don't think I didn't know about the years-long crush you had on him from afar before that. Maybe you knew where he was from, and you were subconsciously drawn there, even though you consciously forgot.'

'I've missed you using your psychology degree on me.'

'I've got plenty more where that came from.'

'Spare me. I only ever knew he was Scottish. Don't forget. I'd never talked to him properly until that one night when I suddenly had a burst of confidence, and we can blame the white wine spritzers at the ball for that. I certainly never got to know him well enough to find out where his home town was or hear his life story. And after he left, I never exactly got the chance.' Back then, Molly hadn't known Ethan's real reason for leaving. All she could surmise was that the connection she'd thought was there clearly wasn't. Something must have happened for him to leave, and he hadn't even bothered to confide in her what it was, so what they'd shared must have meant nothing to him. She'd always struggled to make connections with people, especially after growing up ignored by her parents, so his rejection stung particularly hard, after having liked him from afar for so long. Their perfect night together had raised her hopes only to have them dashed when he left without a word.

So after Ethan, all through university and even into adulthood, all she pursued were fun relationships with fun people, never going too deep, never allowing herself to catch real feelings. Keeping it shallow and safe. Molly wasn't sure Julie had figured that part out yet. So much for her psychology degree.

'Is he still good-looking?'

'It's not about looks,' said Molly. Ethan's beautiful brown eyes and dark lashes flashed through her mind. His broad shoulders and tanned arms and strong hands and long, elegant fingers.

Julie tutted. 'It can be a bit about looks.'

Molly gave in. 'Let me tell you he has aged like a fine wine.'

Julie laughed delightedly. 'So he's a vet, too? Does he live in the village?'

'Yes. Don't hate me but I can see inside his house right now.'

'Molly! Oh, my God, stop spying on that poor man. Are you in the street?'

'No!' Molly burst out laughing. 'I'm in my bedroom. His house is right opposite mine.'

'Oh, that's handy. Can you see into his bedroom?'

After they both stopped giggling, Molly sighed. 'I can, actually. But I promise I've not looked. That would be wrong.'

'Yes, it would. So, is he single?'

'Yes. And he has three kids.'

'Wow, three?'

'Yeah. They're great. They're his little brothers and sister. He's their primary caregiver. It's complicated.'

'Oh. That's a pretty amazing thing to do.'

'Yeah, it is.'

'And they must be pretty amazing, too. I don't think I've ever heard you describe any kid as great before.'

'I'm a changed woman,' Molly joked.

'Sounds it.'

'Just kidding. I'm still the same old weirdo you know and love.'

'I do love you, and you're not a weirdo,' Julie said softly. 'I know you struggle with the thought of turning into your parents. But you know you're nothing like them. You never could be.'

'I guess.'

'I bet you're wonderful with those kids. You've grown and changed for the better, despite how your parents treated you. It would be a shame if you let your whole future be dictated by their views on children and family.'

'Thanks,' Molly whispered back. 'You know, you and Nick should come up and visit me sometime. I have a spare room now.'

'You really are a new woman.'

'I know! I'll even make sure it has a bed and sheets and everything before you come.'

'Maybe after Christmas?'

'Yes, or over New Year's!'

'Oh, that would be fantastic. I've always wanted to spend New Year's Eve in Scotland.'

'Best place for it.'

'Marvellous, I'll tell Nick in a minute.'

'Love that. Not asking him what he thinks, just telling him where he's spending New Year's.'

'Naturally! He doesn't mind where he is as

long as there's a cosy pub and plenty of Guinness.'

When Molly eventually ended the call, she felt lighter and happier than she had in months. She felt something like hope unfurling in her chest. Maybe Julie was right. Maybe she was better than her parents. Maybe she could do this.

CHAPTER SIX

WHEN MOLLY NEXT saw Maisie she was lying on her living room sofa, Kai plumping up a cushion behind her back and Ethan tucking a blanket around her. Molly placed a large bowl of potato salad on the kitchen table, one of the only dishes she knew how to make, as the boys left to prepare for the street party outside. She went back to the living room to see Maisie and perched on the edge of the coffee table to check on her.

'Look at you all comfy. Almost makes me wish I had brothers.' Molly had spent a long childhood wondering what it would be like to have lively brothers she could play games with, or sweet sisters she could share clothes with. Anyone to keep her company, whom she could love and be loved by in return.

'They're not usually like this.'

'I bet.'

'Thank you again, by the way,' said Maisie.

'My pleasure.'

'You literally saved my life.'

'I don't know about that. I'm just glad I was there.'

'Me, too. So is Ethan. He says you're a marvel.'

'He does, does he?' Molly's chest fluttered.

Maisie nodded. 'I think he likes you.'

'Glad to hear it.'

'I mean *likes* you.'

Molly pretended not to know what Maisie meant. 'How are you feeling now? Any pain?'

'They keep saying I've had a shock and I need to rest.' Maisie pulled herself up by grabbing the back of the sofa, and glanced at the door to check none of her brothers were returning. 'Can I tell you a secret?'

'Of course.'

'I'm fine,' she whispered. 'But they keep bringing me snacks and drinks, even without me asking for them. And Harry let me be in charge of the remote.'

'You've never had it so good, huh?'

'Never. I should leap in the path of runaway vehicles more often.'

Molly laughed. 'You'd better be joking.'

'I am. How's your leg, Molly?'

'It doesn't hurt anymore,' she said quietly. 'But do you want to see a really disgusting bruise?'

'Yes!'

Molly showed her the large bright purple bruise spanning her calf, and Maisie seemed appropriately impressed, while also somewhat jealous that she hadn't bruised at all.

Ethan came across and handed Maisie a drink. As Maisie took it, she made a face at Molly as if to say *See?* and Molly tried not to laugh.

'Have you thanked Molly for saving you?'

'Yes, Ethan,' Maisie said, glaring at him.

Molly nodded solemnly. 'She has.'

Ethan left them alone then, but not before he rested his large hands on Molly's shoulders and leaned down to whisper in her ear. 'Thanks for coming to visit her.' He squeezed the back of Molly's neck affectionately as he left, causing shivers to run up and down her spine at his touch.

Molly planned to sit with Maisie for as long as she could, but soon it was time to go home and get changed for the party. Molly was really starting to see how badly her parents had influenced her views on children. She couldn't believe she'd spent so many years dismissing them as something of a nuisance, a presence that would get in the way of a meaningful life, rather than enriching it. Julie had been right; she needed to focus on not letting her parents shape her own views about family.

Suddenly, Ethan's front door slammed open. 'Ethan!' Kai yelled, 'come here, quick.'

Molly jumped up and ran with Ethan to meet Kai, who was closely followed by Harry, holding a cat in his arms.

'We found it lying by the road round the corner by the fields,' Harry said, breathing hard. 'I picked him up really carefully. I didn't hurt him even more, did I?'

Ethan grabbed a towel from the kitchen and reached out to carefully transfer the cat into his own arms. 'Don't worry, Harry.'

'Is it dead?' Maisie cried.

'No, look, it's still breathing,' said Molly. The cat's ribcage was clearly moving steadily in and out, which was a positive sign.

Maisie threw herself at Molly, wrapping her little arms around her waist. Molly rubbed her shoulders and crouched down to get level with her. She pulled her sleeve over her hand and gently wiped Maisie's face, drying away all her tears. 'We'll look after the cat, sweetheart.'

'Is he going to die?'

'We'll do everything we can,' said Ethan. 'We're going to run to the surgery. You three wait here for Aunty Anne.'

Ethan drove them swiftly to the clinic in minutes, throwing his phone to Molly so she could send Anne a quick text explaining what had happened. They rushed into the exam room, where Ethan unwrapped the cat from the towel. 'How's it looking?' asked Molly.

Ethan carried out an initial assessment. 'I think we might be lucky. I'd guess we have one broken leg. He's clearly been hit by a vehicle, but it seems to have been a glancing blow. I don't recognise the cat. He might be a stray.'

There was nothing Molly hated more than people who could hit an animal with their car and then leave them there with no assistance. They gave the cat some pain relief and intravenous fluids.

'There could be bruising to the lungs. We'll have to keep him in, of course,' said Ethan. 'I'll give him blood tests and an X-ray, but hopefully it's just the one fracture in his back leg. Can I have my phone? I want to call the kids, make sure they're okay.'

Molly handed him his phone. He was just as caring and sweet with the animals as he was with the kids. It was very attractive. Molly stroked the sleeping cat while she waited for Ethan to finish his phone call.

130 ONE-NIGHT REUNION WITH THE VET

The cat had no collar, so she quickly scanned him for a microchip, but found there wasn't one.

'What are you up to?' asked Ethan.

'There's no chip. As soon as he's out of danger I'll look after him at home. If no one claims him I'm happy to keep him. He's a sweet little thing.'

Ethan rolled his eyes. 'You really are trying to rescue every animal on the planet, aren't you?'

Molly shrugged. 'Maybe.'

By the time they made it home from the clinic, Ethan didn't have long until the party would be starting. He reassured Maisie that the cat was going to recover and that Molly was planning to adopt him, and she was back to normal in minutes. 'Can I take flying lessons?' Maisie asked as Ethan placed frozen sausage rolls on a tray and threw them in the oven for the party.

'What do you think?' Ethan answered drily.

'Yes?'

'Absolutely no way.'

'What? Why not?'

'You're too young,' said Ethan. 'And even more importantly, it's literally the most dangerous thing you could possibly have come up with. I don't even like the idea of you learning to drive a car in five years, let alone a plane.'

'Molly does it.'

'Yes, she does. And is Molly my little sister?'

'No.'

'Well, you are. And I will do everything I can to keep you safe.'

'You go in Molly's plane practically every day. Why can't I?'

'It's part of my job. I would never set foot in it if I didn't have to.'

'You like it now, though. I've heard you talking about it.'

That made Ethan pause. Did he like it? He'd been so set on hating it that he hadn't even considered the possibility of feeling anything else. But now he thought about it, he had to admit it had a certain exhilarating effect. Take-off and landing were still a little tense, but being up there, seeing the ocean and fields below him, was pretty wonderful. Even a little thrilling. But that didn't mean he wanted Maisie up there.

'Come here,' he said softly.

Maisie folded her arms and glared at him, refusing to move.

'Please, Maisie.' He held his arms open, and after a minute she must have felt sorry for him because she rolled her eyes and stepped reluctantly into his embrace.

'Once you're a grown-up you can do anything you want to do, and I'm sure you'll do it bril-

132 ONE-NIGHT REUNION WITH THE VET

liantly. I won't be able to stop you because you'll
be your own person and your own responsibility. And although that scares me to death, I trust
you to make good decisions. But until you're a
grown-up, it's my responsibility to look after
you and make the bigger decisions for you. Does
that make sense?'

'I suppose.' She paused and thought before
asking, 'When am I a grown-up? What age?'

'Twenty-one?' Ethan took a stab in the dark.

She sighed. 'Great. I'll be an old woman before I get to do anything fun with my life.'

She looked so sad that Ethan couldn't help
what came out of his mouth. 'If you really want
to go up in a plane then maybe I can ask, just
ask, Molly if she thinks it would be a good idea
for us to take you up in her plane one day.'

The screech of joy was directed into his left
ear, and he felt equal parts pain and happiness.
He laughed as she jumped up and down on the
sofa. 'Just *one* trip.'

'Yes, yes, yes!' She continued to bounce joy-
fully.

Part of him wondered what the hell he was
doing letting her try something so dangerous. A
while ago he would have scoffed at the very idea
of it. But he trusted Molly, and now he'd been
up there himself, it just didn't feel as dangerous
as it once had. But while he trusted Molly in the

sky, he still couldn't trust her with his heart, or Maisie's. Ethan was still convinced she would leave when she felt the pull of the next exciting venture abroad. He remembered again their almost-kiss, and felt an equal mixture of frustration and relief that the kiss hadn't happened. His body might want her more than anything, but his brain was insisting on caution.

'So, am I back in your good books?'

'Yes.' Maisie grinned. Then added, 'For now.'

Ten minutes later, Maisie was back in the kitchen. 'Molly's so cool.'

Ethan nodded, trying to read a magazine article about feline hydration, while the sausage rolls cooked in the oven. It was almost time to take them out.

'She's really pretty too, isn't she?' Maisie said.

Ethan looked up from his article. 'Yes?' Ethan answered hesitantly, getting the feeling Maisie was going somewhere with this that he wasn't going to like.

'Do you like her?'

'Yes, we're friends. Do you like her?' Maybe he could change the subject by turning it back to Maisie.

'Obviously. She's the coolest person I've ever met.'

'Yeah, I think you mentioned that.' She'd only

found a way to say it every single day since she'd met the woman.

'I think you should ask her out.'

'I'm not really looking for a partner, Maisie, remember?'

'Why?'

He didn't really want to explicitly remind Maisie about his ex-girlfriend; she was definitely a sore spot for the whole family. 'Well, I'm too busy, for one thing.' He didn't want to mention the fact that even if he was looking, Molly likely wouldn't want a guy with three kids in the house.

'Too busy to go on one date? It only takes an hour to eat a meal.'

'I just… I'm not really looking for romance.'

'Why not?'

'I'm happy just concentrating on spending time with you three and doing my job. That's all I need to be happy.'

'I don't think you are happy.'

'You don't?' Ethan straightened up and put down the magazine. He shifted closer to her. 'I promise you I am. You make me happy.' He bopped her nose and she giggled softly.

'I think you aren't as happy as you could be.'

'I guess if I won the lottery I'd be a little bit happier.'

The doorbell rang and Ethan smiled in relief. Saved by the imminent flood of street party guests.

Various aunts, uncles, neighbours and cousins streamed in over the next hour, leaving bowls and trays of food on Ethan's kitchen counter, and stuffing his fridge full of drinks and meat to grill on the barbecue outside. Molly arrived arm in arm with Aunty Anne herself, giggling about something Ethan didn't even want to ask about. He smiled at the sight of them, heads close, whispering secretively. Sometimes Molly already seemed like one of the family. She fitted right in. Even the kids all liked her, and they rarely agreed on anything. But he still got the sense that she felt skittish at times. As though she still had one foot outside the door. The twins thundered through the house chasing their cousin's white fluffball of a Samoyed into the back garden, shouting hello to Molly as they passed.

A couple of hours later, after Ethan had manned the first shift at the barbecue, and eaten more than his fill of burgers, he headed upstairs to change out of his shirt, which smelled smoky and was covered in grease spatters, then pulled a clean one over his head and joined the others in his living room. There were a few spots free, but he sank into the space next to Molly.

Molly wasn't sure where Ethan had disappeared to, but it was embarrassing that she had even noticed. He'd only been gone five minutes then reappeared in a different shirt. The light blue colour really accentuated his tanned skin and brown eyes. She couldn't help feeling all tingly when he picked the spot right next to her. He lowered his tall frame onto the sofa, and she could feel the warmth radiating off his body, only inches away from hers.

'Maisie said you have something to ask me?' Molly said.

Ethan looked stricken for a moment, but then seemed to remember something and he made a face and shook his head. 'I do. She's got it into her head that she wants to go up in your plane. And somehow, I ended up agreeing to ask you if we could take her up for a quick flight sometime.' He frowned down at his hands. 'Although saying it out loud is making me start to have doubts.'

'No, no, that's a great idea. I'm really proud of you.'

Ethan looked up. 'You are?'

'Yes. You didn't even want to go up yourself on our first flight. Now you're comfortable enough to let Maisie up there with us.'

He shrugged grumpily. 'It's not as bad up there as I thought.'

Molly smiled. He was like a reluctant growling bear. But she found his grouchy protectiveness over Maisie adorable.

'I'll let you tell her the good news next time you see her. I'm surprised she let you out of her sight, to be honest.' Ethan looked around for Maisie.

'She's outside playing with that gorgeous Samoyed dog.'

Ethan nodded and relaxed back into the sofa cushions, his shoulder now touching Molly's. She let herself lean into him a tiny bit, and was pleased to find that he didn't move away.

'Have you had any more thoughts about the D-O-G situation?' asked Aunty Anne.

Ethan groaned and pulled one of the sofa cushions over his face, sinking down into the seat. 'Please don't start bringing that up again.'

'I said it quietly, so none of the kids heard!'

'Very kind of you,' Ethan said drily.

'What's this?' Molly asked, smiling at Ethan's reaction.

'Well,' Anne began, sitting primly on the edge of the armchair. 'I don't know if you heard the terrible news a couple of weeks back, I mean it happened before you moved here, Molly, so maybe you didn't, but sadly a policeman two towns over died in the line of duty.'

'What happened?' Molly was surprised. A police death seemed unusual for such a sleepy place in the Scottish countryside. 'Was he shot?'

'No, it happened on the road. A stolen vehicle crashed into his police car and pushed it off into a valley.'

'Oh, my God, how awful.'

'Terrible. He died immediately.' Anne paused and took a sip from her enormous glass of punch. 'The amazing thing is his police dog was in the car with him.'

'Oh, no.' Molly wasn't sure she wanted to hear the rest of this story.

'No, it has a happy ending. The dog survived with no injuries.'

'Thank goodness.' Molly leaned back in her chair and breathed for what felt like the first time in a full minute.

'And the reason I'm telling you all this is that they've retired the dog from the force, and they can't find anyone to take him on. I know someone who works there. He's a chocolate Labrador, an ex-drug-detection dog, and has the sweetest little face you can imagine.' She sipped more punch. 'Apparently, when he was a puppy, his foster family noticed that he had above-average intelligence and they put him forward for police training. The trainer agreed and he passed his training in three months flat. He was always a bit too friendly for the force, but he was paired up with a police officer and he served them impeccably for ten years. Then the poor thing's owner died in that crash.'

'Aunty Anne, don't you think I've got enough to juggle here without adding a dog to the list?'

'She wants you to take him on?' Molly asked, barely able to hold her smile of disbelief in.

Ethan looked at her quizzically. 'Yes, what's so weird about that?'

Molly shrugged. 'I don't know. It's just hard to imagine a pet-hating vet adopting a dog.'

'Aha!' Anne held up her finger victoriously. 'That's why this dog would be perfect. He's police trained, so he wouldn't be as boisterous as your average dog. Plus, he's getting older now, so he'll be calmer. And the kids have been begging you for a dog for the last nine years.'

'I know.' He sighed. 'And it's not as if I don't feel guilty about it. Especially back when I first got them. Of course they wanted something soft and comforting to cuddle, after everything that they'd just been through. But all I could think about was what if something happened? They'd already lost their parents…what if I got them a pet and then it got sick, or ran away? I couldn't risk it.'

Anne reached over and patted his knee. 'I never realised that was the reason, sweetheart. That makes sense.'

'And I always let them come in and visit the animals at work,' Ethan said defensively, although he seemed to be losing steam and sounding a little doubtful about his decision. 'They're around animals all the time. It's not like I'm refusing them the joy of being around animals.'

'It's not the same as having a family pet of their own, though,' said Aunty Anne. 'Anyway, it's your decision. Just wanted you to know all the information.'

Anne left the room to get more punch. And Ethan scratched his nose and looked over at Molly to find her watching him. 'What?'

'Sometimes it's healthier to take the risk than not take it.'

'Risks? You're one to talk.'

'What does that mean?'

'Nothing. Just that you're clearly not prepared to take a risk yourself by letting kids into your life. And to be honest, I'm not quite sure why you have an issue with that in the first place.'

Molly frowned. How dare he say something like that? He didn't know anything about her life, or her past. 'The risk of taking on an older dog is not the same as committing to a life with children.'

Ethan flinched and pulled away from her. They glared at each other for a long moment, then both seemed to remember at the same time that they were in the middle of a house full of people who could rejoin them at any moment. Some of the tension between them lessened, but it didn't disappear.

Ethan narrowed his eyes. 'Are you going to walk the risk for me when all three kids get bored of it?'

Molly smiled coolly. 'Maybe it can join me and my donkey.'

Ethan shook his head and covered his eyes with the cushion again.

'Seriously though, if you don't want him, and no one else has any plans to, I'll take him.'

'Molly, you can't take in every single waif and stray. You'll have your own zoo soon. You can't rescue everything. Sometimes you just have to be realistic.'

'Forget realistic,' said Molly. 'Why can't I rescue everything? Who makes these rules? It's like when you watch a nature documentary, there's

142   ONE-NIGHT REUNION WITH THE VET

this accepted fact that they mustn't intervene. If a baby rabbit they've been following for a month is about to get eaten by a fox, they have to just document it and let it happen. Well, if I was there, that fox is getting chased off and that baby's getting saved.'

'But then what is Mummy Fox going to feed Baby Fox?' asked Ethan.

Molly snorted a reluctant laugh. 'I know. I get what you're saying. Maybe I'd drop off some nice steaks at the foxes' den. But it's the principle that annoys me. *You can't save everything... you have to let things suffer.* No. You really don't. If you can help, you should help.'

'That's very admirable,' Ethan said. 'Although, what would happen to the animals you take in when you—?'

Molly frowned. 'What? Crash my plane and die in a huge fireball?'

'What? No, I didn't mean that.'

'Then what did you mean?'

'You know. When you decide to…move on.'

'Who says I'm moving on?'

'No one,' Ethan said. But that was clearly how he thought of her. She was just here for now. Just *temporary*. Ethan frowned and looked away, clearly unwilling to carry on the conversation since it wasn't going anywhere. Molly was left with a sinking heart. He was only telling her what she already knew—that she didn't have a good track record of sticking around. Her good feeling after the conversation with Julie trickled away as she lost the confidence she'd found in herself that had told her maybe she could do this if she really wanted to. Did she even want to? When would she know?

As it got darker, they'd moved the party outside to enjoy the decorations. There were fairy lights in all the trees, and the pumpkins had been arranged to line the edge of the road and decorate every front path on the street. Any that were left over were arranged on peoples' front steps or dotted along the tops of garden walls. Somehow, it looked even more beautiful this year than it usually did.

Things were still tense between them since their argument. They needed space away from each other so Ethan retained his distance, but he kept an eye on Molly as his family swarmed around her, offering her food and asking her questions. He knew they could be a bit much. He was back in place at the barbecue before long, and it was time to give the meat one last turn. It would be ready in a couple of minutes. He tried

144   ONE-NIGHT REUNION WITH THE VET

not to stare at Molly, but listened while Kai and Harry peppered her with questions.

'Could you land a plane on the sea?'

'I was briefly trained to use a seaplane, yes. But I've never had the opportunity to try it since. And I couldn't land my usual plane in the sea, unless it was an emergency landing. We would probably sink. Quickly.'

'Can you loop the loop?'

'I can.'

Ethan found that weirdly sexy. Although it would be the opposite of sexy if she ever did it with him in the plane. In fact, she'd better have a good supply of airsickness bags in the plane.

'The Australian guy who first taught me used his plane to herd cattle. You had to do some pretty acrobatic stuff to get them to go where you wanted.'

'Wow. Can we come up in your plane?'

'You'll have to ask Ethan.'

'Could you land on a road?'

'Yes, as long as there were no bridges or power lines.'

'Or traffic.'

'Yep, good call. Cars don't like it when you land on them.'

'Have you ever crashed?'

'Not really. Had a few rough landings. One time I narrowly avoided colliding with a rhino.'

'You're lying!' Kai shouted gleefully.

'I am not!'

'Boys, please, give her a break,' Ethan called out.

Ethan had connected his laptop to a set of speakers in the living room and put them over by the open window facing out. He'd set a playlist of music to play while people hung out in the front garden and over the street, but it was just loud enough to be background noise. He spotted Maisie fiddling with something over by his laptop, and sure enough a few minutes later the volume went up and Taylor Swift blared out.

Maisie jumped up and down in delight, and started dancing immediately in that carefree way kids could still master. Then she headed straight over to Molly. When Ethan saw her grab Molly's hands and try to pull her up from her garden chair, he got up. Molly looked like she needed saving. But before he could reach them, Molly hopped up and let Maisie pull her to a free space, then started dancing happily to the music with Maisie.

Ethan stayed put. Clearly, she didn't need his help after all. He came to a stop by the food table and grabbed a skewer of chicken and sweet potato. As he ate, he couldn't help but watch Molly as she spun around with his little sister, Molly's blond curls swinging around her shoulders. He couldn't bear to think how Maisie was going to feel if, or when, Molly left. He could slowly feel the ground opening up beneath his feet all over again.

Molly danced so easily. If Ethan tried that he'd have someone's eye out, never mind the fact that he'd cause everyone in the area to die from embarrassment. But on her, dancing just looked so natural and cool. People were even joining in. He snorted with disbelief as even Harry and Kai grabbed some of the younger kids and added themselves to the fray.

'She's a special one,' his great-uncle said, nudging a cold beer into Ethan's free hand. 'You literally couldn't wipe that soppy smile off your face if you tried, could you?'

Ethan snorted. 'Very funny.' He hadn't even noticed that he was smiling, but it was true; his cheeks actually ached a bit from it. How long had it been since he'd been made to feel this happy? And just by watching someone dancing for goodness' sake. Seeing her happy, and his siblings happy, made his heart feel like it had grown three sizes. He wasn't supposed to be like this. He was supposed to be concentrating on work and kids. That was it.

The last time he'd felt anything like this was with his ex, Carrie. And everyone knew how that ended. But had he felt as happy as this with her? No, if he was honest with himself—it didn't even compare. Carrie had gotten on well with the twins and especially Maisie, who had taken their break-up harder than Ethan had himself. She'd been sad and quiet for months after Carrie had left. But Ethan was sure Carrie had never quite felt like one of the family, like Molly did. Did that mean that things with Molly could be different? Or did it simply mean that he would fall that much harder when this all went south and she inevitably left? He was terrified at the thought of history repeating itself, with his heart bruised yet again and the kids upset. Should he pull his family back, out of Molly's orbit, to protect them? Or should he have some kind of conversation with Molly about the importance of not letting his kids down? He had absolutely no idea where to go from here. Should he risk everything and just kiss Molly like he longed to, or leave well enough alone?

Dancing with Maisie and the kids had wiped Molly out. Maybe she wasn't quite as fit as she

148   ONE-NIGHT REUNION WITH THE VET

used to be. Or the painkillers she'd taken for her leg had worn off. She sat down in the kitchen, where most of Ethan's family was, to get her breath back.

Aunty Anne and her husband knocked her for six when they joined her and invited her in advance for Christmas dinner. Molly looked to Ethan to see if he looked horrified at the idea. But he smiled and nodded. 'It's a whole big event. There'll be dozens of people there. But plenty of room for you to join.'

Molly's own parents liked a quiet Christmas; they were quite elderly now. They'd never made a huge deal of it, even when she was a kid. It was more about going to church than presents and Santa Claus. She hadn't been able to get home for three out of the past five, and honestly, they hadn't seemed to mind too much. Her parents always went out for a quiet Christmas dinner at the local pub and spent the day with their friends. They wouldn't miss her, and she could always visit in between Christmas and New Year's if they did.

Molly smiled. 'If you're really sure, I'd love to.'

Aunty Anne handed out yet more punch from her seemingly never-ending supply.

'Harry wants to be a vet when he's older, don't you?'

'I want to be an emu farmer now,' Harry said.

'That's unusual,' said Molly. 'I like it.'

'Why did you go off the idea of following in Ethan's footsteps?' asked Aunty Anne.

'I don't want to put animals down. Ethan hates doing it.'

So did Molly. You never got used to it. 'You know, there are other important jobs you can do at a surgery that aren't being a vet,' said Molly.

'Like what?'

'We need someone to come in and help with the overnight stays.'

'What are they?' asked Harry.

'The pets who need to stay overnight so we can keep an eye on them, or for operations and treatment. Studies have shown that animals heal better and faster if they're read to.'

'Read to?'

'Yep, how would you like to come and read to some cats and dogs and rabbits?'

'What would I read?'

'Anything. Your favourite book, a newspaper. They just like the company and the sound of your voice.'

Harry agreed shyly, and Ethan ruffled his hair, looking pleased. Molly was glad she hadn't overstepped the mark inviting Ethan's brother to work. Sometimes she spoke before she thought, but they both looked pretty happy about her idea.

Molly couldn't help but compare Ethan's family to her own. Her childhood had been pretty lonely, and she'd always dreamed of having a brother or sister. This was what she had always imagined having a big family would be like. Always someone to chat to, lots of noise and action and laughter. Everyone stopping by each other's houses with no warning. Everyone on the street was friendly and outgoing. Like *The Waltons* meets *Gilmore Girls*. She never thought she'd live in a place like this. To be honest, she'd never wanted to. She had always valued her privacy. She never really liked to mix social groups together; she would never have spent time with her friends and her family in the same room. She'd always liked to keep things compartmentalised. Maybe because she always felt like she was a different Molly with different people. Fun-loving Molly with her friends, studious, successful Molly with her parents. Who would she be if those people were all together?

But here, with these people, she was just Molly. And honestly, she'd never felt so comfortable or accepted, or more like herself. But there was something big missing. Ethan. After their argument earlier in the evening, she was still feeling a sense of disquiet. She longed to talk to Ethan privately to try to sort it out, make him understand what she was thinking and feeling, although that might be a little difficult when she wasn't entirely sure herself. She was starting to get the sense that she might have been viewing family through the prism of a difficult childhood, but now, through Ethan, she'd seen what being part of a large family could be like. And it was making her rethink everything.

Back at her house alone after the party had dispersed, she lit some candles and gazed out at the street. There were still a few stragglers out there sitting on garden chairs, listening to music at a low volume. She could faintly hear people talking and laughing. The fairy lights still lit everything in a soft glow, coloured light dancing off the dozens of orange and multicoloured pumpkins lining people's garden paths and porches.

Out of the stragglers came a shape, a man walking over the road and up her drive. A decidedly Ethan-shaped man.

'I brought you a peace offering,' said Ethan gruffly, brandishing an armful of boxes at her front door.

'Not more punch?'

He laughed once. 'No. I think Aunty Anne finally finished that off.' He handed Molly three Tupperware tubs in various sizes and shapes.

'Thank you, this is great. You didn't have to do this.'

'It wasn't just that… We didn't really get to say goodbye properly.'

'You came all the way over here just to say goodbye?'

He shrugged his broad shoulders again. 'And good-night.'

Molly put the boxes down on a side table and put her hands in her pockets.

Ethan took a step closer and then hesitated. 'Molly…' he murmured.

Molly closed her eyes against the wave of arousal that hit her when she heard him say her name in that deep voice with a hint of frustration.

Ethan reached out and gently tugged her hands from her pockets, then held them in his, stroking his thumbs lightly over the backs of her hands. She watched as he swallowed, a flicker of indecision in his eyes as he weighed up the pros and cons, before his resolve settled, his desire flared and he smoothly pulled her into his arms. He leaned down and captured her lips in a hungry kiss. Molly moaned into his mouth as he pressed against her. Her hands found their way into his hair, and Ethan's hands seemed to grab anything they could. He gripped her waist, then ran his hands desperately all the way up her back until he cupped the back of her head. He delicately kissed the sensitive skin on her neck and it sent shivers down her spine.

She could happily stay right here and do this for the rest of her life. Suddenly, that thought sent a flash of panic surging through her. She was being too vulnerable. This would turn out to be a mistake; it always did. She couldn't let him do this to her again. She couldn't handle being left by Ethan twice, even if he did have a good reason the first time. She'd been rejected by her parents and then everyone else she'd ever tried, and failed, to connect with. Her panic started to spiral.

It was safer for them to be friends. It made more sense. They had to work together, fly together. He had three kids, for goodness' sake. What did she know about bringing up children? Nothing! She only knew what it was like to fail, with her parents as an example. She couldn't get involved with that. It was too much.

Or was it? Maybe she was wrong.

But it was too late. Ethan had sensed her retraction and he was already pulling away.

'I'm sorry, was that too much?' Ethan asked.

'Maybe. I don't know. I don't know if this is a good idea...'

He looked absolutely mortified. 'I'm sorry, I misunderstood. I won't touch you again.' He took a step away from her, then turned back meeting Molly's eyes. He stared for a moment as if confused by what he saw in them. 'Unless you ask me to,' he said softly. Then strode away, down her path and across the road back to his house.

CHAPTER SEVEN

ON MONDAY MORNING Molly couldn't bear the thought of running into Ethan, so she did the mature thing. She hid.

Molly hid in everyone's favourite room in a veterinarian surgery—the overnight ward. Everyone that was except infamous pet-hating vet Ethan. Of all the places at work, Molly concluded this was the place she was least likely to run into him.

There were two sibling domestic shorthair kittens in the same cage. One ginger-and-white-striped, and one white all over. They started mewing madly as soon as she entered the room. She grinned. 'Hi, babies, you wanna play?'

She had ten minutes before her shift started, and she'd already done all her checks on the plane, which was sitting prepped and ready in the hangar. She unlocked the cage and carefully placed a hand under each tiny warm belly, lifting both the kittens out. She sank down onto the linoleum floor and let them play with the woolly strands on the end of her scarf. She cooed over their tiny ferocious white teeth and little pink noses as they play-attacked each other, then the scarf, then her hand.

Then the door clicked open, and the one person she'd been trying to avoid walked right in.

'What are you doing here?'

She hadn't meant to sound so accusatory, and he frowned, looking grumpy, and reminding her of the Ethan she met when she first arrived. Then he hid his hand behind his back. 'Nothing.'

'What are you holding?'

'Nothing,' he repeated.

'Why are you being so secretive?'

He rolled his eyes and reluctantly brought his hand forward and opened his fist. He revealed a pink cat on a string. 'I got them a new toy.'

He was so sweet. Molly sighed, dismayed that she'd lost that connection with Ethan that had been tentatively growing.

Things were slightly less awkward between them for the rest of the day. But there was still a tension lingering. A wall had gone back up, and Molly wasn't sure how to knock it down. He was being distant and withdrawn, giving her space. Never standing too close, taking care not to touch her. Which was what she thought she wanted. She'd gotten herself into this mess by doubting their kiss. Now she missed the Ethan she was getting to know all over again. She was just trying her best to protect her own heart from getting hurt once more.

The next morning, Molly forced herself to wake up as she loaded her coffee machine and squinted at the buttons. She'd already showered and dressed on autopilot, but she still felt half-asleep. She tapped her radio to switch on the local station and hoped their usual mix of country and pop music would finally break through the fog in her brain, even if it did result in bad music-induced rage. But what she heard woke her up in one second flat. They weren't playing music at all. They were reporting a warning for a big storm headed for the west coast of Scotland. It was coming straight from Bermuda, where it had originated as a hurricane and had already killed hundreds of people.

Molly forwent her coffee altogether as she pulled on her coat and ran across the road to Ethan's house. The grey clouds only sent down a blanket of drizzle for now, but as she squinted into the sky, the tops of the trees were already swaying in a significantly strong wind. Molly flew up Ethan's steps and rapped on his front door.

He answered it whilst talking on the phone, and after a moment of staring, held up a finger to Molly, mouthing, 'One second.'

Molly nodded and stepped inside, focusing her attention on the wall in the hallway, covered in kids' drawings, to at least give the impression that she wasn't listening to his conversation. But she couldn't help hearing every word, since he was standing right next to her and had made no move to step away. She couldn't help but relive their kiss in her head. The taste of his lips and the feel of his hands in her hair.

She tried to take her mind off it. She concentrated on his phone call. She could almost hear the voice at the other end. Not enough to make out words, but enough to recognise it as Jon.

'Yeah, it's heading in fast,' Ethan said into the phone, then paused to let Jon answer.

'I heard ninety-mile-an-hour coastal winds, with hundred-mile-an-hour gusts.'

Ethan waited then replied again. 'Worst storm we've had in years, decades maybe. Hopefully, the house will be okay, our street is so protected, but I want to board up the windows at the surgery, at least the big ones that face the ocean, since it's coming in from the west.'

He nodded at Jon's response. 'Okay, I'll be over there soon.'

He hung up the phone. 'You heard about the storm?' Ethan was still a little distant, but Molly could see that he was trying to focus on the matter at hand. She realised with a pang that she might have done too much damage for them to ever recover a good working relationship again.

'I thought I'd left extreme weather behind me.'

'No, it can get pretty bad up here. The schools are closing for the day, so I've dropped the kids off at Aunty Anne's. I don't want them home alone. So now we need to head to the surgery and, well, I'm sure you heard the rest.'

Molly attempted to smile. 'You caught me.' Her smile wasn't reciprocated, so she switched to being practical and professional, ignoring her bruised heart. 'Does this happen a lot?'

'We've only resorted to boarding up windows once before. That had to be five…six years ago now? But they reckon this storm will be worse.'

By the time they arrived at the surgery, Jon was already outside with a stack of plywood boards and a tool kit by his feet. The wind was a lot sharper and colder now they were near the ocean.

160 ONE-NIGHT REUNION WITH THE VET

'Maybe we should close for the day, except to emergencies. What do you think?' asked Molly.

'Yeah, good idea,' said Ethan. 'I'll get Lara to postpone any nonemergency appointments, then I'll send her home.' Molly started helping Jon while Ethan rushed inside to do just that.

'Watch out for splinters,' Jon said as they each grabbed one end of a sheet of plywood and propped it up on the sill below the first window.

'I should have brought my gloves.' As Molly eyed the ancient hammer Jon fished out of his old toolbox, she wished she'd brought her tools as well. Her dad, as distant as he was, had always taught her to get the best quality equipment she could realistically afford, whether that was a stethoscope, a spanner or a casserole dish. Either way, she just hoped Jon's hammer would last till they got this place boarded up.

Ethan reappeared. 'Lara's a star. I told her she could go home, but she wants to stay with the pets. Keep them company, make sure they don't get scared.'

'Have I ever said how much I love her?' asked Molly.

Ethan laughed a little, despite himself. 'She's one of the best.'

Molly held the board in place, pressing the edge down as firmly as she could, and gazed at Ethan as he concentrated on the job at hand. Hope began to spark inside her that maybe Ethan could forgive her for hurting him and giving him mixed messages. He made quite the picture as he hammered nails in, hair whipping against his face. He squinted against the freezing rain, holding the next nail between his teeth, and heaved the next board into place, hammering the last few nails in carefully to secure it.

'That'll have to be good enough.'

Ethan burst into the staff room where Molly was making coffees and trying to warm up next to the radiator. 'We got an emergency call from Winnie. But Jon couldn't understand what she was saying. All he got was that maybe a wall has come down, and some animals might be injured or trapped.'

Molly dropped her spoon onto the counter. 'Let's get going.'

'We have to let the storm blow over first. There's nothing we can do now.'

'Of course there is. We can get to her and help the animals now.'

'We can't fly in this, Molly.'

'I've flown in much higher winds than this.' Molly wasn't sure that was precisely true, but she'd certainly flown in winds equally as strong.

162   ONE-NIGHT REUNION WITH THE VET

Yes, it had been a little treacherous, but she was a good pilot; she'd landed the plane. And she could do it again.

Ethan stared out at the storm clouds and the trees bending in the wind. 'We can't.'

'I can.' Molly grabbed her keys and pulled her jacket on, then rushed out the door, only to be stopped by a large, firm hand on her arm. He immediately pulled it away as if she'd burned him. Molly rolled her eyes. Was he seriously keeping that stupid vow of not touching her, even now?

'Molly.'

She pulled her hair out from underneath the collar of her jacket and stayed close to him, so he could hear her shout over the noise of the wind and rain. 'I understand that you can't risk it. You have kids to look after. It makes sense for you to stay here. But I don't. I can't leave Winnie on her own. She'll be outside in this trying to save the animals herself. You know she will.'

Molly left Ethan standing in the rain and strode towards her plane. Her mind was already racing with the route and what she would do to make sure she landed safely.

A moment after she slammed the plane door shut and grabbed her headphones, the passenger door opened and Ethan jumped in, along with a shower of rain and wind.

'Obviously, I'm coming with you.' He grumpily grabbed his shoulder harness and clicked it into place.

Molly wiped the rain from her face and stared at him. The swell of relief she felt that he was joining her shocked her, but she didn't know what to say when things were still so strange between them. So she fell back into the bickering they'd recently gotten used to. It was much easier to understand. 'Don't do me any favours.'

He avoided her gaze and glared through the windscreen. 'Let's just get going.'

She studied her GPS nav/com screen. 'The storm is travelling west to east. From Winnie's farm towards us. It's already hit her and left. I'm going to try to fly around the worst of it, then approach Winnie's farm from behind the storm. We should be fine.'

As confused as Molly still was over what had happened between them, for a moment she had to fight to keep a smile off her face. Not just because she wanted him with her, but Ethan joining her meant that maybe he was losing some of that fear of taking risks he'd built up over the years they'd been apart. Which gave her double the reason to make absolutely sure nothing happened to him. She was going to precision fly this plane and give him a textbook landing if it was the last thing she did. And despite that unfortunate turn of phrase, she tucked away her feelings, turned the ignition and started taxiing out onto the runway.

'You might want to close your eyes. This is going to be bumpy.'

CHAPTER EIGHT

ETHAN HAD JUST started to get used to flying, was maybe even beginning to enjoy it. So it was a terrible time to experience a storm. All the ease and confidence he'd built up inside Molly's plane went right out the window as they climbed closer to the ferocious charcoal clouds.

In any case, his worries about the storm took second place to his preoccupation over what had happened with Molly. He was still mortified about the kiss, and hurt that she'd rejected him. He hoped the whole mess hadn't hastened her desire to leave. He was almost grateful to the storm for providing a distraction so they wouldn't have to talk about it.

He hadn't realised how much they touched day to day, how close they had gotten in such a short space of time. Trying to avoid that touch was a full-time job in itself. Making sure to take one step away from her every time they were in the same room. Being careful not to touch hands when he passed her something at work. And most difficult of all, avoiding bumping shoulders or thighs when they were trapped in the plane together. But he had to continue to try. He wanted her to know that they could work together even if she wasn't interested in him. He couldn't risk chasing her away. He didn't want to be the reason she left even earlier than she was probably going to. Her pulling away had only cemented that feeling. The other reason was less important but all encompassing. He knew that one touch would drive him crazy, and if she was the one to pull away it would put a crack in his already bruised heart. He sighed and reminded himself that he'd recovered from romantic disappointment once, with Carrie, and he could do it again if he had to. Even though, deep down, if he was honest with himself, he knew he was in far more trouble with Molly than he'd ever been with Carrie. And that was probably a sign that he should have held Molly at an even greater distance right from the get-go.

They flew around the storm without too much turbulence. Ethan saw flashes of lightning in the distance, far enough away that it didn't worry him too much. And when they reached the now familiar runway by Winnie's farm, they both looked down to see what damage had occurred.

At least five trees had come down, and everything looked like it had been thoroughly thrown around. But at least from their viewpoint, the house and major outbuildings still seemed to be standing.

They landed bumpily, Molly making sure to avoid the stray branches that lay all over the field, having been torn off the trees by the gales. They came to a stop, jumped out of the plane and rushed towards the farm.

Molly was right; the worst of the storm seemed to have passed. But freezing-cold rain still lashed down unrelentingly, and the wind was constant, with gusts that almost made Ethan lose his footing.

They tried Winnie's house first. Ethan rapped his knuckles on her front door with no response, then knocked on the kitchen window. Molly pressed her face against the glass, cupping her hands around her eyes to block out the reflections. 'She's not in there.'

'You head that way, I'll go this way and we'll meet around the other side,' instructed Ethan. He and Molly split up, and he ran through the courtyard towards the hay barns and the outbuildings. The place was a mess. Hay bales had blown down and were scattered all over the place, distressed cows were wandering freely and chickens huddled in corners together, trying to keep warm. A trailer had blown over and was lying on its side. There were several roof tiles missing, and the top of the chimney was missing entirely, but at least the rest of the house looked undamaged. But where the hell was Winnie? Ethan's chest tightened.

Ethan shouted Winnie's name, but his voice was whipped away by the wind. Then he rounded the corner. First, he saw Molly, then he followed her shocked gaze. What had once been the front wall of Winnie's stables was now a huge pile of brick-red rubble. And there was Winnie, right on top of it.

Molly was right, as usual, and Winnie had taken it upon herself to save her animals singlehandedly. She had climbed up onto a pile of bricks and was tugging them up and throwing them onto the yard behind her. She stopped momentarily to push her wet hair behind her ears and happened to catch sight of them. He thought he saw a flicker of relief on her face before she admonished them. 'You flew here? In this weather? Are you crazy?'

'It's smoother up there than it looks,' Molly shouted over the sound of the wind.

Ethan held his tongue, but you could have fooled him. If the pilot had been anyone other than Molly, he'd never have set foot in that plane. He jumped up and joined Winnie in grabbing bricks and tossing them out of the way. 'Who are we looking for?'

'Twenty head of sheep and my two Gloucester Old Spot pigs. I moved them inside the stables for safety. Then the wall fell in, blocking the doors. If they die, it's all my fault.'

'They won't die,' said Molly, climbing up to help.

'You can't promise that, Molly,' warned Ethan.

They all fell silent and concentrated on tackling the rubble. For a few minutes, aside from grunts of exertion, all Ethan heard was the wind and rain, the lowing of confused cattle and the occasional bleat from the sheep inside. At least they knew some were still alive in there, if not uninjured.

Ethan pulled some more wet bricks out, and finally made a hole through to the stable. He crouched down to peer through. 'Looks like they're all huddled together on the undamaged side. If we make this hole bigger, I can drop through and take a closer look.'

'We don't want you getting injured as well,' said Winnie.

'I'll be fine.' Ethan untucked his T-shirt and

used the dry end to wipe his soaking wet face. It would help if he could see properly.

'Just don't fall on one of the sheep, for God's sake,' muttered Molly quietly.

She scraped her hair back, now dark brown it was so wet, and somehow twisted it into itself and tied it into a knot on the back of her head in one practiced move.

'Oh, I was planning to aim for one for a soft landing,' Ethan said drily and equally quietly. She grinned at him. He smiled back, pleased that at least they were managing to put aside their own conflicts and work well together in the face of this disaster. His heart lifted for a moment before he sternly reminded himself that Molly had already given him a very clear indication that anything more than a professional relationship between them was off the table. And he had to respect that.

They slowly made the hole bigger, until Ethan could climb down and drop the few feet to the ground. It felt marginally warmer down there, thanks to the straw-covered floor. He smiled at Winnie's two pigs, both fast asleep. One sheep bleated at him inquisitively, and he worked his way through the flock, checking each one as best he could. Twelve sheep and seven lambs, seemingly safe and well. That meant one was missing.

'You said twenty sheep?' he called in the direction of the hole.

'Yes,' answered Winnie. 'How many do you see?'

'Nineteen. Just hold on a second.'

One of the sheep he'd already counted was standing away from the others, sniffing and pushing at the fallen bricks with her nose. Ethan rushed over and carefully moved the bricks, trying not to cause a Jenga-like collapse. Underneath, he found a bucket of feed and the twentieth sheep. A young lamb had managed to end up in a pocket of space between the bucket and the fallen bricks. Ethan thought he was unharmed, but as he got up, he bleated and limped towards his mother, favouring his front right leg. Ethan cursed softly and picked him up before he made it worse by walking on it.

'I've got an injured lamb,' he called up. 'But everyone else seems fine.'

Molly and Winnie had widened the hole farther and Ethan passed the lamb gently up to Molly. 'Winnie, how about you take him indoors and keep him warm, and we'll get the others out. Watch his leg.'

One by one, Ethan passed up each sheep and lamb to Molly and she set them free into the courtyard. The pigs were a little more difficult, and Ethan ended up making a sling out of his sweater. With a lot of manoeuvring, everyone got out safe. Ethan scrambled out last.

Winnie had managed to herd all the sheep into the barn where they could stay and keep warm for a while. She poured some food into the trough inside, then insisted Molly and Ethan come in the house for a hot drink.

Ethan could use one. He was soaking wet and cold, and the adrenaline from helping twenty-two animals through a hole in the roof was starting to wear off.

The wind howled around them as they rushed indoors to the safety of Winnie's kitchen. It was a relief to close the door behind them and shut out the weather outside.

Ethan joined Molly at the kitchen table where he could feel the warmth from the fireplace crackling in the corner. It was a huge kitchen, but the yellow walls and warm oak furniture gave it a comforting, cosy feel.

Ethan noticed the lights were on. 'You didn't lose power, then?'

'I lost it when the storm started, but it came back on not long ago. I've always got the generator if it goes off again.'

'Do you have plenty of food? Do you need anything?'

'Trust me. I'm set for an apocalypse.'

The injured lamb sat on a blanket on one end of the huge wooden kitchen table. It bleated at Ethan mournfully. 'I know, little man. Let's get you fixed up.'

He gave the lamb as thorough an examination as he could. 'I suspect his metacarpal bone could be fractured.'

'Do you want to take him back to the surgery with us?' asked Molly.

'Can we take him in the plane?'

'Sure. I'm planning to make the plane more accommodating to take emergency cases to and from surgery at some point. But this time he'll have to travel on your lap. Can you handle that?'

'I think I'll manage. In the meantime, let's make him a splint for the journey.' Ethan helped the lamb sit back down on his blanket, where he seemed fairly happy to stay. 'Winnie, do you have a spare cardboard tube from a roll of kitchen paper?'

Winnie nodded. 'I'll get you one.'

While Ethan gave the lamb an injection of painkiller, Molly pulled out some cotton wool and a roll of pink vet wrap bandage from her bag and passed them both to Ethan. He wrapped the lamb's leg carefully in cotton wool, then cut down the edge of the cardboard tube, fitted it around the leg to keep it straight, then wrapped it well with the vet wrap. The bandage was designed to only stick to itself so he didn't need to fasten it with anything. 'There. That should do until we get him back to the surgery.'

'Your roof is going to need some work, and the chimney,' said Ethan.

Winnie sighed. 'I saw. God knows where I'll get the money for that.'

'I know my way around a roof, and I know a few people who'll want to join me,' said Ethan, thinking of his surgery coworkers plus a few practically minded neighbours whom he knew wouldn't want to leave a local in need without help. Since Molly and her plane had come along, distance meant less. Winnie felt like as much of a neighbour to him as the people next door on his own street. Their circle of familiarity had widened. Ethan wondered what would happen to this newfound sense of community if Molly left. He would definitely make sure to talk to Jon and encourage him to find a new pilot if that were to arise, because even if it wasn't Molly, it was clearly a service their vet practice needed to provide. But it felt terrible to think about it not being Molly.

'I helped build a surgery from scratch in Zambia,' Molly piped up. 'I'm pretty good with a drill and a handsaw.'

'You're both very sweet,' said Winnie. 'But I'm not sure if this might be a sign.'

'A sign of what?'

'That it's time I retired.'

Ethan and Molly shared a look as Winnie placed a steaming mug of coffee in front of each of them.

'What would you do instead?'

Winnie sighed. 'I always wanted to pass the farm down to one of my boys. But as I mentioned before, neither of them are interested. I used to hope they'd carry on after me and run the place, or have children who'd want to, but no. I swore I'd never sell a stitch of land to a developer, but there has been one sniffing around, and now I'm wondering if it might be best.'

'I know what it's like being stuck with a house that needs work.'

Molly looked quizzically at him. 'But your house is lovely?'

'It's a little small for us now, plus I'm pretty sure the whole roof needs doing. It's not urgent, but it's always hanging over my head, knowing I'll have to get it done sometime. There's just always something else that needs doing first.'

176 ONE-NIGHT REUNION WITH THE VET

'With three kids, I'm not surprised.'

Ethan and Molly spent the time it took to drink their coffees trying to help Winnie brainstorm different solutions to her problem. But really all it came down to was finding someone to buy the place and take it on as it was, warts and all, or letting a developer have it. It broke Ethan's heart to think of the whole beautiful property being flattened and turned into a huge house estate or a golf course.

After washing his and Molly's mugs in the sink, Ethan told Winnie it was time they got the lamb back to the surgery.

'Thanks for all your help,' Winnie said. 'I couldn't have done it without you.'

'It's what we're here for.'

'Wait. I'll get you some milk for the lamb.' Winnie quickly prepared Ethan a bottle of milk with a teat.

'Thanks. We'll get him back to you as soon as we can.'

Ethan scooped up the lamb and tucked it inside his coat, before stepping outside where they were soaked to the skin within seconds.

'It feels like it's gotten worse again.'

'It's just a squall,' said Molly.

'Are you sure you don't want to fly back with

us and wait out the storm there?' Ethan asked Winnie.

'No offence, but there's no way I'm getting inside that thing. Besides, I don't want to leave the animals. I'll be fine. I've been out here for far worse storms.'

Ethan could believe it. She'd been living out here for decades. He felt bad leaving her, but she insisted that was what she wanted, and to be honest, despite trusting Molly implicitly, he wasn't entirely convinced Winnie wouldn't be safer at the farm than in a plane in this weather.

'Maybe we should stay, too.'

Molly, to give her credit, didn't disagree immediately. She looked up at the sky for a long minute, searching for what, Ethan didn't know. But after taking in the clouds and the wind, and doing some kind of calculations or pilot magic in her brain, she shook her head. 'No, I think I can fly underneath it.'

'Underneath it?'

'The lightning's stopped. I think the safest route is beneath the storm.'

Ethan shrugged, ready to put his life in her hands yet again and just be done with this day. 'Okay.'

They sprinted to the plane, and Ethan supported the lamb snugly in one large hand as he used the other to grab the door frame and pull himself into the aircraft. Once in his seat, he grabbed the seat belt then settled back. 'You cold, little man?' He pulled the lamb more firmly against his chest and wrapped his scarf around it, tucking it in gently. He could feel its little heartbeat thrumming against his chest.

And soon, Ethan's was doing the same. When Molly had said she'd fly under the storm, she wasn't joking. After take-off, she'd hardly climbed at all. It was certainly exhilarating but at one point Ethan swore she had to pull up to avoid an electricity pylon, and that was when he realised he was holding the lamb a little too tightly. He relaxed his hand and stroked the lamb's head in apology with one finger.

The storm clouds were dark, and lightning was still visible in the distance. Rain lashed the windscreen, and wind buffeted the plane from side to side. They hit what Ethan had to assume was some particularly strong turbulence, and the plane wobbled violently. The lamb bleated, then he heard a small pop from the direction of the engine.

'What was that? Is the plane all right?'

Molly tapped one of the dials on the control panel and flipped a couple of switches. 'Okay, don't panic.'

Ethan's stomach dropped. 'What's happened?'

Molly didn't answer, but clicked on the radio and stated her call sign. 'Oban Traffic, Skyhawk six-two Delta.' There was no answer, only a steady crackle on the line. She quickly barked, 'I think I've lost the engine.'

A bolt of lightning lit up everything and re-vealed to Ethan the sickening realisation that the propeller was completely still. Only then did he notice that the engine noise had stopped alto-gether. An eerie silence filled the plane. Ethan's blood ran cold, but after a moment of pure panic, an inexplicable wave of calm hit him. He took a deep breath. 'Can I help?'

Suddenly, the engine made a loud cracking noise that even Ethan knew it wasn't meant to make, and he could smell the unmistakeable scent of smoke and oil.

'Damn.' Molly got back on the radio. 'I don't know if anyone can hear me, but my engine's gone. We've lost power and there's smoke in the cockpit. I'm going to have to find somewhere to set down immediately.' She gave the position of the aircraft and turned to Ethan.

'We're not going to suddenly fall out of the air or anything. I'm just going to glide us down slowly.'

180   ONE-NIGHT REUNION WITH THE VET

Ethan scanned the ground beneath them. 'Down to where?'

Molly checked her dials and screen constantly as she spoke. 'There are no airports close enough, and I can't see a straight piece of road. I'm going to head to this patch of flat ground here—' she tapped the screen swiftly '—and set us down.'

There was another flash of lightning and Ethan couldn't help but think of Kai, Harry and Maisie. Who would look after them if he died? He knew Aunty Anne would probably step in. She was so maternal, and she'd offered to take on the kids right back at the beginning, but Ethan had refused. The kids would be with him and no one else. He'd accepted her help while he finished his degree and been grateful for it. But if they lost him, too, he was pretty sure the kids wouldn't come back from it. He should never have gotten in the plane with Molly, or allowed her to come out here in the first place in this storm.

'Don't be scared. You know I wouldn't let anything happen to you.'

'Or your plane, I know.' It was very sweet of her to try to comfort him even mid-emergency landing, so he tried to make a joke and flashed her a smile, which probably came off more as a grimace. He carefully tucked the lamb farther inside his jacket, then zipped it up around him. He supported the lamb with one hand and gripped the armrest with the other. 'Is there a brace position for a small plane?'

'Your shoulder harness will keep you from hitting your head on the panel. Cross your arms in front of you, and keep hold of our passenger,' Molly said tightly.

Ethan nodded.

They descended quickly, and in the lightning flashes it was clear that they were surrounded by fields, no buildings to hit, or roads to crash into. Hopefully, no one else could get hurt, whatever happened.

'Brace,' Molly said firmly.

Ethan pushed himself back in his seat and crossed his arms over his chest, keeping the lamb in place and making sure not to crush him between his chest and arms. He held his breath. They hit the ground hard and bounced twice before setting down. They seemed to be travelling too fast and for too long, so Ethan glanced over at Molly.

'We're okay. Hold on.'

They finally came to a stop, nose almost in contact with the hedge at the far end of the field. She'd landed perfectly and Ethan had never felt

182 ONE-NIGHT REUNION WITH THE VET

such a strong combination of relief, exhilaration and to be quite honest, attraction. Molly was a goddess. A goddess who was currently ripping off her harness and jumping out of the plane into the storm. Ethan unclenched every muscle in his body by force and checked on the lamb. The ridiculous thing was fast asleep.

Ethan grabbed his bag and jumped out after her. She was by the engine, which was still slightly smoking and covered in a black patch in one corner. The smoke stopped as they stared at it.

'Damn it.' Molly hit the side of the plane with her palm flat, then looked like she regretted being so mean to her beloved plane.

Why was she angry? She'd just delivered the most miraculous emergency landing Ethan could ever imagine witnessing. She'd saved all their lives with her talent and expertise.

'Are you okay?' asked Ethan, shouting over the sound of the rain.

'Yes,' she snapped.

'Am I okay?'

Molly glared over at him, her eyes flashing, but he caught a moment of intense relief on her face as she ran her gaze down over his body, checking for injuries. 'You look fine. And your friend. We have to get out of here and find shelter. There's no point in me taking the casing off and looking at the engine until after this storm.'

'Was it the storm? Were we struck by lightning?'

'I don't think so. I won't know till I can take a good look. Maybe rainwater got into the fuel tank and blew it.'

It was getting dark, but due to the terrifying flashes of landscape Ethan had seen on the way down, he was pretty sure he knew exactly where they were. The ocean was on their left, and he was sure he'd spotted the tiny shape of Otter Island just off the coast. That meant they were near a place he knew well. A moor that he'd spent a lot of summers hiking on.

'I know where we can go. Follow me!' he shouted.

CHAPTER NINE

ETHAN FOLLOWED THE line of a river he recognised. It was usually a peaceful brook, but tonight it had turned into a cascade of rushing water. They struggled through whistling wind and rain that pelted them in the face for half an hour, then Ethan stopped and grinned in victory as he spotted the small stone structure exactly where he'd expected it to be.

A one-storey stone building sat nestled between the trees. An ancient bothy, one of many that were scattered throughout the Scottish countryside. The bothies lay empty and were a haven for any walkers who were beset by bad weather or needed a place to stay the night. He'd stayed in this one before, but just for an hour or two until the rain stopped, never overnight. He was impressed that he'd remembered the location so well. It had been a while since he'd found the time to get out and hike, especially once the kids weren't interested anymore.

He unlatched the door, slipping clumsily with wet hands, and held it open for Molly. Once inside, he dropped his medical bag and pushed the door shut against the wind, locking it closed, and leaning against it, suddenly exhausted.

The bothy was old but remarkably well built. The noise of the storm was quieter now, and no wind seemed to be getting in through any cracks in the doors or windows. There were dark stone walls and a wooden floor, and if they didn't find a way to light the two fat half-melted candles on the table, it would soon be too dark to do anything.

'Give me the lamb.' Molly held out her hands and he gratefully passed him over.

Molly started to get together a bed for the little thing, and Ethan had a quick look around. There were two rooms in the bothy, the main room and a very basic bathroom off to the side. Most bothies didn't even have that, so they were lucky. The main room had an old wooden table and three chairs, and a fireplace at the other end, with a pile of dry wood stacked neatly next to it, all ready for burning.

'The last person to use the bothy left fuel in here, thank God. I thought I'd have to go searching for dry wood somewhere.'

And next to the fireplace sat one solitary double bed. Two mismatching pillows and a small pile of blankets sat on top neatly folded. He turned resolutely away from that discovery and pulled open his bag. 'Please let me have a lighter in here,' he mumbled.

Molly carefully placed the sleeping lamb inside its makeshift bed on the table and cleared her throat, then threw him a lighter as if from nowhere.

He piled some of the logs in the fireplace and ignited the lighter. They soon had a crackling fire, giving off much needed warmth and casting a cosy orange glow over the whole room.

Ethan tried his phone, but as he'd suspected there was no signal. Molly's was the same, and as she put her phone back in her bag, Ethan noticed something.

'Molly, you're bleeding.'

She looked down as if surprised to see the small patch of blood soaking through her sleeve. Then she shrugged. 'It's just my arm.'

'Well, you only have two of them. Come here.'

She shrugged off her soaking wet coat and draped it over a chair then let him softly tug her close. It was the first time they'd really touched since their kiss, but Ethan was more worried about her arm than keeping strictly to his promise.

He rotated her arm gently and found the source of the blood. A graze on her elbow.

'You must have knocked it when we landed.'

'I didn't even notice.'

'Must be the adrenaline.'

He wouldn't need much of his medical kit. First, he cleaned the cut with iodine-soaked cotton wool. He dabbed as gently as he could, but Molly still let out a small hiss. He covered the graze with a square antiseptic pad, then wrapped a bandage around her arm several times and fastened it securely.

All done, he finally looked up and found her face closer than he expected. When he eventually dragged his gaze away from her full mouth and looked into her eyes, he found he couldn't look away. 'You've really been getting into trouble lately, haven't you?' Ethan whispered.

She tilted her head in that adorable way that meant she was confused.

'Your leg, now your arm,' Ethan continued.

'Lucky I've got you on hand to patch me up every time.'

'Always.' Ethan smiled. He took a deep, fortifying breath, reminding himself that Molly didn't want him, and forced himself to leave her side. 'Stay put. I'm going to make you some food and a hot drink.'

'Where are you getting food from?'

'I always have food. I look after three kids.'

'Fair point.'

Ethan was pleased to spot a box of teabags someone had left behind on the shelf above the table. He looked closer and found they'd also left some instant soup mix that was still in date. Probably a better choice than the child-friendly snacks and granola bars he had in his bag. He boiled the kettle over the fire and made them two mugs of soup, which they both devoured hungrily.

'Now, I know how this sounds, but we've really got to get out of these wet clothes.'

Molly snorted.

Ethan rooted through his bag and tried to control his body's physical reaction to her by sheer force of will. He pulled out a hoodie and a woollen hat. 'These are all the spare clothes I have on me.' He threw the hoodie towards Molly's good arm, and she caught it. 'Take off your wet things and put on that and some of the blankets. We'll hang up our clothes by the fire and they'll be dry before we know it.' Ethan turned and grabbed a blanket for himself.

'Where are you going?' asked Molly.

'I'm going to change in the bathroom.'

Molly rolled her eyes. 'You don't have to

run away. You won't turn to rock if you see me naked.'

It was Ethan's turn to snort.

'Oh, very mature,' said Molly.

Ethan shrugged. 'I'll stay here if that's what you prefer.'

Ethan turned away from Molly. She was damn well going to get some privacy whether she cared about it or not. He was a gentleman. He swore under his breath as his new position gave him an accidental view of Molly changing in the reflection of the window. He averted his eyes and concentrated on not falling flat on his face as he pushed off his boots and tugged down his wet jeans. Mercifully, his boxers were dry, so he left them on and peeled his soaking sweater and T-shirt off over his head.

Molly tied a scratchy blanket around her waist like a sarong, and sent up a debt of gratitude to any gods who might be listening that she had thought to shave her legs earlier. Not that she should care, since nothing was going to happen between them. In fact, it would be far better if they looked like a forest, then she might not be so tempted to throw herself into his arms.

She pulled on Ethan's hoodie and was pleased to find that it smelled like him. She took in a deep breath; it was soft and warm, just like Ethan. She had to admit it was sweet of him to give it to her, especially when all he had left for himself was a woolly hat. Trying to get comfortable on the bed, Molly pushed a pillow against the wall and leaned back into it, the fire still keeping her feet warm.

Which fortunately, or unfortunately, gave her a front-row seat to Ethan stripping off all his clothes. Fortunately, because he was absolutely beautiful and somehow already had his jeans off. Unfortunately, because it was not doing her attempts to keep away from him any favours at all.

She stared up at the ceiling for a moment.

Stay strong, Molly, she told herself. *If you can help an injured elephant give birth without so much as a stethoscope, and scare off a pair of chimpanzee poachers using a mobile phone in your pocket as a fake weapon, you can resist one perfect, beautiful man in a cosy, cramped bothy where there is only one bed.*

She watched his slim waist broaden into wide shoulders and muscular upper arms as he pulled his clothes off. She watched the muscles flex under the honey-coloured skin of his back as he pulled the shirt and sweater apart and leaned over to drape them both over the chairs near the fire. She remembered every detail about his body last time she'd seen it, in microscopic detail. His twenty-one-year-old body had been gorgeous, but it wasn't a patch on his fully grown mature one. It almost took her breath away how much he had changed in the past nine years.

He turned as he slung a large blanket over his shoulders and pulled it around himself, and Molly swallowed hard as she briefly saw the muscular planes of his chest and hard stomach. She knew he didn't have a spare minute of time to work out in a gym, so that body was simply an accidental side effect of the hard work of being a vet, spending time outside and lifting heavy animals all day long. And a naturally fit body had always been her particular weakness. Why was she trying so hard not to do something she really wanted to do? She suddenly couldn't remember.

Ethan joined her on the far end of the bed and carefully laid back, but since the bed was small and the only spare pillow was right next to her leg, she suddenly found herself with half a lapful of Ethan's head. He smiled up at her. And she tried to calm her racing heartbeat.

'Comfy?' she asked drily, trying hard to disguise her inner feelings. She really needed to snap out of it. He was off-limits. And that was down to her and her own reservations. She'd chosen to pull away and she needed to stick to it. If she took that step, if she gave in and made love to him again, she might not ever be able to leave him.

'Very much, thank you,' said Ethan. 'Is this okay?' He gestured at himself and the bed in general.

She rolled her eyes. 'Of course it is.'

She couldn't bring herself to move away and create a couple of inches of space between them. She needed the extra warmth, she told herself.

The pillow hid Molly's leg so as he wriggled into place, getting comfy, he unknowingly moved his head farther onto Molly. 'I hope the kids are all right.'

'Didn't Anne say she'd watch them?' asked Molly.

'Yes. But Kai hates storms. He's never normally one for displays of affection, but storms are the only time he comes to me for a cuddle.'

Molly slapped her hand to her heart. 'That's so adorable.'

'Yeah, he's not as tough as he likes to pretend.' Ethan glanced up. 'Don't hate me, but part of me secretly loves it when I hear thunder. I don't want him to be scared, but at least I get to hug him.'

This family was going to be the end of her.

She gazed down, admiring Ethan's deep brown eyes. His long black lashes cast shadows over his cheeks in the flickering light from the fire. A lock of his hair fell out of place across his forehead, and she couldn't help pushing it back into place. 'Do you want your hat?' she asked softly.

He shook his head, and her fingers caught in his hair. The little details about the reality of having three growing kids were endlessly surprising to her. She was impressed all over again at how Ethan had managed to overcome all the odds and provide a stable home for his siblings, despite being so young himself. It was admirable. She wondered how she would have coped under the same circumstances when she found it so hard to stay in one place for any length of time. But seeing the bonds that Ethan and his siblings shared, it was starting to dawn on her that some sacrifices were well worth making. She knew he wouldn't change his situation even if he could.

His skin felt warm under her cold fingers, and she found herself carding her hand through his soft, thick hair, still damp from the rain but warm in her hands. It gave her something to do, and distracted her from thinking about the storm and how her plane was doing out there.

Ethan's eyes drifted shut as she stroked through

his hair softly. 'Will your plane be all right outside?' he asked as if reading her mind.

Her heart melted further at him still caring about her plane's well-being.

'I won't know what happened to the engine until the morning, but she should be okay,' Molly answered. 'I'll check on her at first light.'

'Are all planes shes?'

'They can be whatever you want them to be.'

Ethan looked up at her again. 'She's very beautiful.'

As Ethan gazed into her eyes, she wondered if he was still just talking about the plane.

'If you're trying to get on my good side by complimenting her…it's working.'

Ethan laughed. He sighed softly as Molly's hand stroked through his hair. 'That feels good.' He closed his eyes. 'You really are an amazing pilot, you know.'

Warmth spread through her chest at the compliment. 'I'm not bad.'

'Not bad? You saved my life. We could have died.'

Molly wasn't so sure about the first part. But she didn't want to tell him how right he was about the second. Landing with no power, in such low light, on an unpredictable, rough surface, any number of things could have gone wrong. Catastrophically wrong. They could have hit power lines, a hedge, a tree, or even a herd of cattle. They'd been very lucky. She felt terrible. 'Ethan, I'm sorry for insisting we come out in such a bad storm.'

'No.' Ethan touched her wrist and made eye contact. 'It was worth it to make sure that Winnie was okay.'

Molly nodded.

'Did you always want to be a pilot?' Ethan asked.

'Not from the beginning. I always dreamed of running a sanctuary. But then I realised I couldn't do that and travel at the same time. Then while I was in Australia, that farmer taught me to fly his plane, and I suddenly had a new dream.'

'You really love travelling, don't you?'

'I like discovering new places. I never would have seen a stampede of zebras migrating across the Serengeti or been in a Jeep attacked by two hippos if I'd stayed in England, I guess.' She had loved travelling. It used to be all she thought about. Where hadn't she been yet? Where would she like to go next? But Molly wasn't sure if she might have had enough of new places. She was starting to wonder if she might have finally found the place she'd been searching all over the world for.

'You must miss all that adventure,' Ethan murmured.

'Sometimes,' she answered, noncommittally. 'What made you decide to be a vet?' Molly asked as she suddenly realised she had no idea.

'When I was a kid my uncle's cattle farm came down with bovine tuberculosis. Hundreds of animals killed just like that,' he said, snapping his fingers. 'It was awful. It was the first time I'd seen my uncle cry. Or any man in my family, I guess. That's when I knew what I wanted to be.'

'Wow. Sorry, Ethan.'

Ethan shrugged, then smiled. 'I know why you wanted to be a vet.'

Molly raised a doubtful eyebrow. 'Go on, then. Enlighten me.'

'You want to save everything. You never met a living being you didn't want to save. Butterflies, ants, birds, donkeys.'

Molly laughed, but didn't disagree.

'So what would this dream sanctuary be like, then? Did you plan it out?' asked Ethan.

Molly settled back into her pillow. 'I'd buy a really big plot of land. And I'd take in all the abandoned animals that have nowhere to go. Farm stock that was no longer viable, or no good for breeding. Injured animals. Anything anyone no longer wanted. And I'd give them all a safe, happy home for the rest of their lives. However long or short that might be.'

Ethan's smile grew. 'Yeah, I can see you doing that. If I die and come back as a donkey, I'd happily live at your sanctuary.' He stared up at the ceiling, avoiding Molly's gaze. 'I felt like me and the kids could have used somewhere like that, back when everything happened.'

Molly's heart broke a little. It didn't seem like it at the time, but when she looked back at them in college, they hadn't been adults. Ethan had still been practically a kid himself. She was reminded again about what Ethan had been through, dealing with losing his mother and figuring out how to take responsibility and provide for three young kids.

'Obviously, we weren't abandoned on purpose,' Ethan added. 'But that doesn't make much difference when you're feeling alone and scared. I always try to protect them from feeling like that again. Which can make things tough sometimes. You know, relationships end. The kids feel unwanted again. Anyway, it was a pretty rough time.'

'Of course it was. You say I saved your life, but you saved theirs. All three of them. That's way more heroic than knowing how to land a plane.'

'I guess we're both a couple of heroes.'

Molly laughed. 'I guess so.' She glanced over to the table to check on the lamb, who was still blissfully fast asleep. Suddenly, Ethan shot up from her lap and scrambled to sit farther away. Molly's heart leaped out of her chest. 'What? What is it?'

'Nothing. Sorry. I just realised I was on your lap.'

Molly rolled her eyes. 'Oh, for goodness' sake, Ethan.' He was serious. He really was never going to touch her again unless she asked. Molly regretted ever having let him say something so stupid. And to be quite honest she was getting sick of the whole thing.

Ethan reclined opposite her at the other end of the bed. His apparent cool exterior annoyed her. Especially with all the inner turmoil she was currently experiencing. All because of him. The gorgeous idiot. He leaned back on one elbow and let his legs stretch out on the bed. He was trying to fit politely around her body, but the bed was so small that his long limbs couldn't find anywhere to go. She could feel the heat from his body as he tried to get comfortable. He was one of those people who always looked at home in his own skin. So even here on this threadbare bed in an old stone cottage, his hair all mussed up, wearing a blanket, for goodness' sake, he managed to look like a model in a fashion magazine.

He was frustrating, and tempting and so beautiful she suddenly wanted to cry. He'd been so vulnerable with her, and now she felt almost closer to him than she could bear.

She wanted Ethan to touch her. She couldn't think of anything in the world she wanted more. To feel his hands on her face, for him to press his hot honey skin against hers, to taste his beautiful mouth on hers. But he'd made it very clear that she was going to have to use her words and damn well ask him. And that might just be the most terrifying challenge she'd ever faced.

'We'd better get some sleep,' said Ethan.

She would definitely ask him. Just not right now.

'The sooner we sleep, the sooner morning comes and the sooner you can check on your plane. I know that's all you're thinking about.'

Yeah, that and wanting your tongue in my mouth.

Her eyes widened as that thought jumped into her head unbidden. And she shook her head to get rid of it.

'Do you want to top and tail or…?' Ethan asked.

'No! We're not twelve. Just lie down here.'

'Okay, okay.'

They climbed under the covers, Ethan taking the side of the bed next to the wall and making sure Molly had at least her fair share of all the blankets.

'You warm enough?' Ethan asked.

Molly nodded and they both settled down side by side, lying on their backs. She couldn't help but be reminded of the last time they'd shared a bed. It felt like a lifetime ago, when they'd both been two very different people. The fire cast the room in shifting orange light, and the only sound was the wind and rain outside. Molly had never been more aware of her body, and how close it was to Ethan's. She catalogued every millimetre of her skin that was in contact with his. Their shoulders were just touching, and she could feel his arm grazing her hip as he breathed in and out. This was torture. She closed her eyes and listened to him breathing softly. The sound was comforting, and eventually it soothed the squally mess in her head.

She somehow drifted off to sleep, only to wake sometime later, in the pitch-black. She could no longer hear the crackle of the fire, and her feet were freezing. But her body was cosy and warm, and she slowly realised why. They had somehow both shifted position in their sleep and now they were facing each other. Her head was comfortably cushioned on Ethan's biceps and his other arm was draped protectively over her waist. She felt safe, cocooned snugly by his warm embrace, and there was nowhere she would rather be. He moved his arm minutely, and tingles ran up and down her spine.

She looked up at his face in the moonlight and gasped. Ethan's eyes were open. He blinked sleepily.

'Hi,' he whispered.

She felt like she'd been waiting a whole decade to be this close to him again. There was something about the darkness, the intimacy of the moment, that made her say something she might never have said in the light of day. 'I never stopped thinking about you,' Molly whispered.

'Neither did I.'

She reached out a hand and laid it gently over his cheek. He leaned into her touch like a cat, and she rubbed her thumb over the soft skin under his eye and pulled him close. Close enough to feel his breath on her lips.

'For the love of God,' she whispered. 'Please touch me.'

Their lips crashed together as Ethan surged forward. He wrapped his arm around Molly's shoulder and pulled her close, until she could almost feel his heart beating through her chest.

Molly sank into the kiss and ran her hand through his hair, the silky strands slipping easily through her fingers. His free hand found hers between their bodies, and he slid his fingers in between hers, gripping her tight. When they paused for breath, Ethan ran his hand softly up her arm leaving goose bumps in its wake. Then she pressed her head back into the pillow as he kissed her jaw, his hot mouth moving slowly down her neck, pressing kisses all the way down her throat to her collarbone.

It was even better than the last time they were together. He had a man's body now. All firm muscle and smooth planes, and strong arms holding her to him, and large, practiced hands that knew exactly what they were doing. Touching her just right, pulling her in, gripping her tight.

'Are you sure you want this?'

'I want this. I want you,' she breathed.

'Then I'm not leaving this bed until I've tasted every inch of you.'

CHAPTER TEN

ETHAN WAS WOKEN at dawn by a soft bleat. Everything that had happened last night came back to him in a rush, and he realised Molly was still in his arms. Which was probably the only reason they hadn't expired from the cold. The fire must have gone out hours ago. He couldn't help but wonder what would happen when Molly woke up. Maybe she would emotionally withdraw from him again, put her barriers back up. He hoped not, but he knew the happy bubble they were in couldn't last forever. Maybe nothing had changed. Maybe she was still just as likely to leave as she ever had been. But there was a tiny spark inside him now that was allowing him to hope. Rather than jump up and get the fire started again, he snuggled down under the blankets and pressed closer to Molly, partly to steal some of her body heat, but mostly to follow his instincts and get as close to her as humanly possible. She grunted adorably, still fast asleep, and unconsciously wrapped her hand around his wrist.

After enjoying their closeness for as long as possible, Ethan knew he had to check on the lamb. He slowly extricated himself from Molly's grip and tested their clothes. They were finally dry. He quickly pulled his jeans and sweater on, then checked on the lamb. His blanket had kept him warm, and his splint was still in place. Ethan fed him the spare bottle of milk that Winnie had provided and gave him a quick cuddle.

'You two are so cute,' Molly mumbled from her pillow.

'It's about time you joined the land of the living,' Ethan said.

Molly yawned and stretched, thrilled to hear her clothes were dry. Ethan noticed that she kept his hoodie and pulled it on again over her clothes.

They both tried their phones again, but there was still no signal.

'I hope the kids won't be too worried about you,' said Molly.

'If I know Aunty Anne, she will have covered for me. They won't know anything's wrong yet. I'm sure she will suspect we simply stayed at Winnie's until after the storm. I really need to get somewhere with a signal, though.'

'I guess we probably should have stayed at Winnie's,' Molly said contemplatively.

Ethan shrugged. If they'd stayed at Winnie's, none of what happened last night would have happened. And he was not mad about it. He made Molly some tea, thrilled to be stuck alone in a bothy with the most beautiful woman in the world. But he had to be careful. Until she was prepared to have a conversation about their future, he couldn't assume anything.

As they ventured outside into the early-morning light, they saw for the first time what the storm had done to their surroundings. Fallen trees and scattered broken branches as far as they could see. They left the bothy as they'd found it, minus a couple of packs of instant soup, and plus a few granola bars.

Once they found the plane, they discovered the trail of destruction behind it. Carnage from where they'd touched down all the way to where they finally came to a stop. They'd busted through three small bushes and left two very visible, deep lines through the crops and grass. The nose of the plane was inches from an old oak tree growing from the middle of the hedge that Ethan hadn't even noticed last night. 'Glad I didn't hit it.' Molly ran her hand over the trunk.

Molly walked around her plane a couple of times inspecting the damage. She magicked a screwdriver from her bag and unscrewed the casing on the engine. She poked around while Ethan stepped back and kept quiet, stroking the lamb's head.

'Well, the engine's done for. I think water got into the fuel during the rainstorm.'

Ethan winced. 'Sorry.'

'I can replace it. Plus, she's got a lot of scratches and scrapes from the landing, but I think everything's repairable.'

'Can she fly home?'

Molly shook her head. 'Definitely not. I'll have to come back out here with a mechanic and fix her later. Or, if not, hire some transport that can tow her home.'

'Talking of home, how are we going to get back?'

'How do you feel about hitching a lift?' Molly asked.

'Fine, as long as you promise to fight off any serial killers.'

'It's a deal.' They shook hands, and Ethan took the opportunity to pull her in for a soft kiss.

'I'm glad your plane survived.'

'Me, too,' she said and hugged him tightly around his waist. He buried his face in her soft blond hair. The intimate moment was only interrupted by a mournful bleat coming from inside Ethan's jacket.

They hopped up on top of a farmer's gate on the grass verge at the side of the road and sat next to each other, waiting for a vehicle to pass their way. It felt like now might be a good time to attempt to draw Molly into having some sort of serious conversation about their relationship. Ethan took a deep breath and prepared himself for Molly's walls to go back up; he knew he had to approach this carefully.

At this point, the main thing was to get them both home safely. Pushing her for a commitment when they were stranded and she couldn't escape from the conversation would be unfair of him, and might be too much for her.

'I really enjoyed last night.'

He was relieved when Molly smiled shyly. 'Me, too.'

A goofy smile spread itself over Ethan's face whether he wanted it to or not. 'I won't lie. I've been wishing that could happen again for the last nine years.'

Molly smiled, then gazed into his eyes. 'There's something else you want to say, isn't there?'

Was he that obvious? 'There is something I

wanted to talk about, yes.' She waited patiently for him to continue. 'It's about the kids. I know you know this, but they've had a pretty rough childhood up to now. I can't really put them in a position where they are likely to get hurt again.'

'Hurt how?'

'By people they've grown attached to leaving them.' Ethan maintained eye contact, waiting for her to understand.

'Oh. You mean me.'

Ethan nodded.

'They're attached to me?'

Ethan smiled. 'Of course they are. My whole family loves you.' *And so do I*, he found himself thinking. The sudden realisation made him feel unsteady on the gate, and he tightened his grip on the railing.

Molly stared into the distance, her forehead wrinkling with concentration. 'I would never want to hurt them, Ethan. My own childhood, well, it wasn't great.' She paused for a moment. 'I was a mistake. My parents never planned to have me. My mother thought she was too old to fall pregnant. They weren't great parents, and they didn't really know what to do with me. All they cared about was working hard and making money. So they treated me like a burden. I grew up thinking that's what children were.'

Ethan put one arm around her and squeezed her shoulder, encouraging her to continue.

'I've always been a bit lonely, you know? I only really came into myself for the first time at university. I got that first taste of freedom and never wanted to let it go. That's why I became a pilot, I think. So any time I want I can get away from everything and fly free.'

Ethan pulled her closer to him. 'That makes a lot of sense.'

Molly put a hand on Ethan's knee. 'So, I guess that's why I've always thought I'd be bad with kids. I didn't want to become my parents.'

Ethan put his hand on top of Molly's. 'I think you're looking at this all wrong. I think your experiences can help you be amazing with kids. You know exactly what not to do. You know exactly how not to treat them.'

'Maybe.'

Ethan carefully jumped down off the gate, making sure not to shake it, and turned to Molly. He stepped closer and wrapped his arms warmly around her shoulders, pulling her close and holding her tight. 'Thank you for opening up to me, Molly.'

She pulled him closer. 'I feel better having told you,' she said.

Ethan smiled and pressed a kiss into her hair.

Maybe this was finally a sign that she might be ready to move forward with him, or that she might consider it at least. His tiny spark of hope glowed a little bit brighter.

After a long day, which started with finding their way home with a lovely farmhand named Michael, and ended with booking a plane mechanic, reuniting Ethan with the kids, who as he suspected hadn't known anything was even amiss, and getting the lamb treated properly and settled in the overnight ward, Molly hadn't had much time to think about what had happened between her and Ethan. She almost never talked about her childhood. After all, who wanted to tell people they were a mistake? But she'd felt strangely lighter after sharing it with Ethan. Maybe now he would understand that she might never be able to give him what he needed from her. He'd sent her home early to get some proper rest, but now she was alone, the doubts were beginning to creep back in.

Her phone interrupted her emotional spiral, and she was excited to see who it was.

'Julie!'

'How's tricks? Anything to share?'

'Well, actually…'

'Oh, my God, what's happened?'

Molly suddenly felt nervous. She wasn't entirely sure how Julie would react. She nervously fiddled with a pen and doodled a heart on a page in her notebook. 'I may have spent the night with Ethan.'

'Wow.'

'Yes. And this time I am relieved to report that he did not run for the hills.'

'Ah, well, that's a relief. But I never had any doubt.'

'You didn't?'

'Who would want to run away from you?'

Molly made a face. Try everyone? 'Anyway, I doubt you called just to talk about my love life.'

'Regrettably not. I'm reluctantly calling you to tell you something.'

'Oh, no, don't tell me you can't come for New Year's anymore?'

'It's nothing to do with that. I'm reluctant because I don't think I should tell you this, but I promised I'd tell you if anything came up.'

'Can we start again? I don't think I've had enough coffee yet for this conversation.'

'Nick's setting up a new project, and there's a position for you if you want it.'

'Oh, wow. Where?'

'Romania. They're setting up a lynx rescue. Building it from the ground up. It's at least a six-month project, maybe longer.'

'That sounds…interesting.' It did. Any time

212 ONE-NIGHT REUNION WITH THE VET

in the last decade she would have been all over it. Would have jumped at the chance to drop everything and go and start a new adventure. She'd always wanted to see Romania, and lynx were beautiful. One of her favourite wild breeds. But…

'You didn't want to tell me?'

Julie seemed to pause carefully. 'I think you're happy where you are.'

Molly wrote the offer down on her notebook. Writing things out on paper always helped her think them through.

Job offer. Romania. Lynx rescue. Six months or longer.

'Don't be in a hurry to decide,' said Julie. 'Nick says there's no rush.'

For the first time in her life, Molly didn't know what she was supposed to do. She was a free spirit. She wasn't meant to stay in one place. When she was growing up, lonely and ignored, she'd promised herself that she would always fly free. Talking to Ethan had brought back all her doubts. If she wanted to be true to the real her, she should go. Right? Ethan appeared to be giving her the right signs, the feeling that he wanted more with her, but how could she be sure when she'd made so many mistakes in the past? And this time there were three vulnerable children in the mix. What would happen if he got tired of her, if he found her lacking, or went off her like all her other partners had? After having opened up to him, she was suddenly feeling exposed to him in a way she hadn't been with anyone else. She felt the almost irresistible urge to do what she usually did and move on, but something inside her was telling her to stay and fight.

But should she really listen to that inner voice when it had steered her wrong so many times before?

'I'm just not sure whether there's anything keeping me here, Julie.'

'I think there is.'

A little while after Molly hung up, her doubts crept back.

Would anything have happened if she and Ethan weren't stranded together, sharing a bed? Was he really interested in her, or was she just in the right place at the right time? Was she just kidding herself that they'd always had something special? Maybe he'd sent her home because he was sick of the sight of her and didn't know how to let her down gently.

Across the street, Ethan sat on his porch, gazing out through the pools of orange light from the streetlamps. His phone rang, and after looking at the caller he picked it up.

'Do you need us again?' asked Ethan.

'No, no,' said Winnie. 'Stand down, soldier. Just calling for a chat.'

Ethan settled back into the swing seat and put his feet up on the coffee table. 'How are the animals doing?'

'All good. How's my lamb?'

'He's doing great. He's staying overnight at the surgery, but rest assured he's getting a lot of attention from everyone.'

'Glad to hear it. You can't keep him, you know.'

'Tell Molly, not me. She loves him. Your electricity is still okay?'

'Yes, everything's fine.'

'I spoke to Jon about your roof. We're getting some people together. We're hoping to drive out at the weekend and get it all fixed up in one day. Would that work for you?'

'I'm hardly a social butterfly. I'll be here whenever you can come. I'll be stuffing you all full of food and drink and treats, I hope you know.'

'That's why I'm coming.'

Winnie laughed. 'Now, listen. I called for a reason.'

Ethan had suspected as much.

'I've been thinking more about the farm. I decided I do want to give it up. But not to developers. I want it to go to a family.'

Ethan was relieved. 'That sounds perfect. It should be a home, not a golf course.'

'I quite agree.'

Ethan still wasn't sure why Winnie was calling him in particular about this. 'Did you want some numbers for estate agents? I can look some up for you.'

'No, I don't need them. I have another idea.'

Ethan suddenly realised he might have figured out why she'd called him. 'Wait, just so you know, I cannot afford to buy your farm. I couldn't afford it, Winnie. As much as I'd love to. And I would love to. You know I think it's beautiful out there.'

'That's not quite what I have in mind. I don't exactly want to sell it at all.'

CHAPTER ELEVEN

MOLLY WAS ON the phone when Ethan knocked on her front door. She stared at him for a moment, then beckoned him inside.

'Take your time,' Ethan whispered. 'I can wait here.'

She nodded, held a finger up to him to denote she'd only be a minute and scampered upstairs, still holding the phone to her ear.

Ethan waited in Molly's living room, buzzing with anticipation. As soon as he'd finished his conversation with Winnie, he knew what he had to do. And he suddenly couldn't wait to do it. It was time for him to trust Molly with his heart and take the biggest risk of his life. Yesterday, after they'd spent that remarkable night together, being so open with their bodies and their feelings, Molly had finally opened up to him about her past. Everything that had stood between them made sense to him now. And he knew they could overcome all of it. If only they both wanted it. And now, he was sure she did.

He'd seen Molly interacting with his siblings. She clearly cared for Maisie and the twins, and now he knew more about her past, he was sure he could support her growing confidence with them.

He could faintly hear Molly's voice from upstairs over the noise from the street outside. Someone's car alarm had been going off down the road for the past few minutes, and he tried to tune out the annoying noise.

Ethan's phone vibrated in his pocket and he took it out to find a message from Maisie. He was needed at home. Kai had set off the fire alarm trying to cook. That was what that noise was. He crossed to the window and pulled Molly's blinds up. There was no smoke visibly billowing from his house, at least. He'd have to run over and check on them. But it would be quicker to leave a note for Molly rather than wait for her to finish her phone call. He looked in her kitchen and saw a notebook lying on the counter next to the fridge.

But as he read what was written on the first page, he felt his lungs seize.

Job offer. Romania. Lynx rescue. Six months or longer.

His heart pounded so hard he felt sick. He

218   ONE-NIGHT REUNION WITH THE VET

knew it. She was leaving him. He felt the disappointment crushing him.

He was such an idiot. He'd known this would happen; he'd told himself time and time again not to get attached, not to let the kids get attached, because he knew she would do this.

There was a tiny heart drawn in biro underneath the note. Clearly, she was excited to go. And he could hardly blame her. Of course Romania and lynx were more exciting than being in the middle of nowhere in Scotland. With him. Of course Molly didn't love him like he loved her. He knew now for sure that he was truly and passionately in love with her. It wouldn't feel this crushing if he wasn't. It had always been her, ever since university. He'd never forgotten her, never been able to get her out of his head no matter how much time passed.

He couldn't deal with this right now; he had to check on the kids. The idea of leaving Molly a note forgotten, he headed for the door.

'Where are you going?' Molly's voice rang out, an audible smile in her voice. Ethan's hand was already on the front door handle. He froze, not turning around.

'Nowhere. Just home. That noise you can hear right now is my kitchen fire alarm going off.'

'Oh, I thought it was just a car alarm.'

Ethan turned the door handle and pulled it open. 'I have to get going.'

'Are you okay?'

Ethan swallowed. He knew it was strange that he hadn't looked at her yet, and that she could tell something was up, but if he turned and looked into her eyes, he wasn't sure he would be able to pretend he didn't know about the job offer. He couldn't act like he hadn't just found out something that had made his entire world fall from beneath him.

The fire alarm fell silent in the stillness between them.

'I guess they figured it out without you,' said Molly carefully.

Even the kids didn't need him. Ethan breathed in once, then let it out. 'When are you leaving?' he asked quietly.

Ethan heard Molly step closer to him and he gripped the door handle tighter.

'What are you talking about?'

'Don't pretend with me, Molly. Please?' Ethan finally turned. 'I saw the note.' He gestured in the direction of the notebook, still sitting on the counter. But she didn't look. She obviously knew what he was talking about now.

Her gaze dropped to the floor. 'I haven't decided if I'm going yet.'

Ethan nodded, not sure what to say.

'I knew you would do this,' Ethan said, more to himself than to Molly. 'It's not even your fault. You can't help it. It's just what you do.'

Molly's eyes snapped up to his. 'What do I do?'

'You move on. You never stay in one place. And I knew that from the start. I can't compete with years of conditioning from your parents, convincing you that you have to keep seeking out excitement wherever you can because you can't find fulfilment inside yourself. You don't recognise when you have something of true value right in front of you that's worth more than a brief shot of adrenaline.'

'Oh, really? And why do you even care?'

'I just thought maybe you'd changed, finally grown up, perhaps.'

'Is there something wrong with how I was?'

'No! I just thought maybe you were ready to—'

'Settle down? Is that what you were going to say? Not everyone wants to settle down. Not everyone wants to have a mortgage and two point four children.'

'Believe me, I know that,' Ethan said.

Suddenly, he felt transported back to when Carrie had left him. But this was so, so much worse. He felt infinitely more for Molly than he had ever felt for Carrie. He hadn't meant to, but he'd let himself imagine Molly becoming a permanent member of his family. He shut his eyes for a moment to process the pain. He'd always feared this would happen. No woman could ever want him as he was, with the commitments he had to his family. And he'd never, ever swap them for any woman, not even Molly, as much as he felt for her. Her words stung so much he could no longer bear to ask her to stay; he needed that decision to come from her. At least Maisie hadn't been around to hear it this time. He couldn't bear to think about how he was going to explain to her that this had happened again.

Molly looked stricken, like she knew precisely what he was thinking.

'What exactly would I be staying here for? You know me so well, you tell me?'

Ethan thought desperately. 'You love your job. You're helping people. You get to fly. You love flying.'

'What else?'

'You have a house, a home of your own. You never had that before.'

'And?'

Me, he wanted to say, you have me. But he couldn't bring himself to say it and get rejected by the only woman he'd ever really wanted. He couldn't let down that last, final barrier and expose all his vulnerability to her. He felt stupid now for having thought she would or could change. 'Listen, I get it. I get why you want to go on an adventure to a new place, to build something new. I guess I just hoped...'

'Hoped what?'

'That building something new with me might be enough,' he answered quietly. He couldn't look at her while she rejected him; he couldn't even listen to the words she was about to say, so he quickly carried on talking. 'I'm sorry for what I said to you about your parents. I'm only angry with myself, not you.'

'I should hope not. I haven't done anything. What would you even be angry with me for? Living my life? Putting myself first? I don't have anyone else to think about. I never have. No one's ever been interested.'

Ethan frowned. He had to accept that she'd never actually promised him anything. It was all just hope that he'd built for himself. It was time to do some damage control for his pride's sake. He took a deep breath.

'I think you should go. I think it's the right decision.' He met her eyes. 'I was wrong to ask you to consider staying. We don't need you here. I'm sure you'll be happier in Romania.'

She suddenly looked like she'd been slapped. Her face closed down, and her emotions shut off as Ethan turned away.

Ethan had finally stepped through the door he'd been glued to and walked away. And she'd let him.

All she'd wanted was for him to ask her to stay. But she'd been left disappointed. *We don't need you*, he'd said. He couldn't make it any clearer than that. He hadn't asked her to stay. Even Ethan couldn't love her. All her past failed relationships rattled through her head. She wasn't enough for any of them.

She'd thought Ethan might be different, but he was just another person who could see that she was unlovable and inadequate as a life partner. He probably knew she'd be useless as a joint caregiver to his siblings. She was going to miss them so much.

She knew he'd be fine without her. This was what she did; she was the person people dated before they found the one. Judging from her history, the next woman Ethan dated would be the one he married. She shuddered; the thought of Ethan with another woman felt like being stabbed in the heart, so she scrubbed the idea from her mind.

224   ONE-NIGHT REUNION WITH THE VET

* * *

In the morning, Molly called Julie to tell her she was accepting the job. But halfway through the conversation, something made her ask Julie a question.

'When you called me, you said you thought there was something keeping me here. You meant Ethan, right?'

'No, I didn't.'

'What, then?'

'I meant you. You are keeping you there. I think you've finally found what you've been travelling the world looking for.'

'What?'

'Yourself. Your new self. For the last few years you loved going to new places, doing new things, moving on. And some people might spend their lives happily doing that forever. But not you. I think you're done. I think you're ready for your next adventure. And that's staying put. Finding out all the amazing things you can experience in one place.'

'He didn't ask me to stay,' Molly said quietly.

Julie paused for a moment. 'Did you really give him a chance to?'

Maybe she hadn't given Ethan a chance. Maybe she'd pushed him away to protect herself.

'And to be honest, is that really the most important thing?' Julie continued.

'What?'

'You should stay for you, not just for him. Do you want to stay?'

That was the question. Maybe she could finally open her animal sanctuary in Romania. Or maybe after this one last job she could start again somewhere new. Every country in the world had unwanted animals she could save. The world was her oyster.

But the thought of starting her sanctuary without Ethan by her side left her cold.

Suddenly, she noticed the boxes of food Ethan had brought her that night, still stacked on the table by the door. She'd forgotten to put them in the fridge. As she got closer, she noticed something sitting on top of them. A purple woollen glove. She recognised it immediately. The night they'd spent together at uni, he'd left behind his T-shirt, but he'd also left behind the glove he lent her to keep her warm that night he'd split the pair, one glove each. She'd lost track of hers over the years; this must be his. She picked it up and held it against her hand. He'd kept a memento of her, too. All these years.

CHAPTER TWELVE

ETHAN SAT ON his porch, watching over Maisie as she played in the garden, digging up weeds from the flower beds with her bright pink trowel.

He spent most of his time gazing furiously at Molly's house, telling himself it was better to feel cross than admit his heart was breaking. He wondered if she was in there packing. He tortured himself with how depressing it would be to look over there in a few days when she was gone. Or in a few weeks when someone else lived there. What the hell was he going to do without her? He could feel the hole she would leave in his life already and she hadn't even left yet. He knew it was time to warn Maisie about what was happening. He beckoned her over, and she joined him on the swing seat, jumping on his lap.

'I don't want you to feel too sad, but I wanted to tell you that Molly got a job offer in another country.'

'She's going?'

'I think so, yes. I'm sorry. We'll all miss her, but like I told her, she needs to follow her dreams. We all do.'

'You told Molly to go? Are you an idiot?'

'Maisie!' The kid had never reminded him more of Molly. 'It was for her own good. She'll be happy there.'

'She was happy here.'

'Yes, I think she was.' Ethan sat back and wrapped his arms around Maisie. 'I guess that means you might not get your trip in her plane. I'm sorry, sweetie.'

'That's okay.'

'It is?'

'Are you okay?' Maisie twisted around and looked up at him, full of concern. And he realised how grown-up Maisie had gotten lately. She wasn't crying or shouting about Molly leaving. She even seemed more worried about him than about losing out on her plane trip. He hugged her close. Maybe the kids weren't as delicate as he thought.

His thoughts returned to Molly again. He wanted Molly in his life. Carrie's leaving didn't define his worth, or control his ability to be loved again. And Molly was nothing like Carrie. Even the kids knew that. He thought of the look on Molly's face when he told her to go. Hope suddenly sparked as he realised he hadn't given her the chance to have her say. Maybe if he'd worded things differently she might have opened up to him, too. Maybe he jumped the gun? He'd jumped to old conclusions about her, about himself. It was time those preconceptions changed, for both of them.

Molly opened the door of the clinic and Ethan held out a bunch of wildflowers. She stared at them, frowning.

'They're from my garden. Maisie helped me pick them.'

'They're very beautiful.'

'Maisie said you can feed them to the donkey if you want. I made sure they're all edible.'

Molly snorted a short laugh. 'I might just do that.'

'I was wondering if I could talk to you for a minute. If you're not busy.'

She gazed at him for a moment. Ethan wanted to pull her close and never let go, but everything felt delicate, like he could say the wrong thing and lose his mooring at any moment. 'You can come with me to feed the donkey,' she said.

Molly led the way through the clinic and out the back door. She made her way through the yard and out to the stable behind the building. The donkey ambled out to meet them, and Molly held the flowers over the fence and let her munch on them.

Ethan smiled and rubbed the donkey's head. 'I was wondering if you'd mind flying somewhere with me today.'

'Do we have a job?'

'No, it's not a job.'

'We can't just fly off, Ethan. We have work.'

'No, we don't. Jon gave us the morning off.'

'What on earth for?'

'If you come with me, you might find out.'

'Why are you being so mysterious?'

'Come on.' Ethan smiled. He gave the donkey one last pat and held out his hand to Molly. She stared at him, the corner of her mouth twitching and threatening to turn into a smile. She rolled her eyes, left the rest of the flowers behind for the donkey and followed Ethan all the way to the hangar.

The plane looked good after its recent adventures, if a little rough around the edges. Jon already had an aircraft mechanic on standby to help keep the plane in working order for their patients. Which meant that he'd been able to get her picked up and her engine replaced quickly.

'Doesn't she look great?' Molly asked, running her hand gently over the fuselage.

'She does.'

'There are still some nicks and scrapes that need repairing before she's back to perfect condition. But I want to tackle those myself.'

'She's okay to fly?' Ethan checked. His plan would be pretty useless if she wasn't.

'Yes! It'll be her new engine's maiden flight.' Once they were both strapped in, Molly looked over at Ethan. 'Where are we headed? You're going to have to tell me something, unless you want to try flying this thing.'

Ethan laughed. 'Not a chance. Just fly north.'

'Ethan!'

'Okay, okay. Head to Winnie's farm.'

'Why?'

'Only one way to find out.'

She shook her head and started to get the plane ready. Ethan grinned. It was time to be brave for both of them and take a risk. Only this risk didn't even feel scary anymore.

The farm looked completely different from the last time they'd been there. Its lush green fields stretched out under the cold blue sky. She was so happy to be spending time in such a beautiful place. She'd travelled all over the world, but she could honestly say the rugged Scottish landscape was her favourite. She'd be lucky if she could spend the rest of her days flying over it.

They landed smoothly, and Molly wasted no time ripping off her headset and jumping out of the plane.

'So what are we doing here? No more stalling.'

Ethan took her hand, and they started walking slowly towards the farm. 'If you are going to Romania, I want you to know that I fully support that. But I was thinking that maybe in six months, when you've saved all the lynx, you might want to come back home…to me.' He looked at her, and she blinked back, nonplussed. 'Only thing is,' he continued, 'home might look a little bit different then.'

Molly frowned. 'What do you mean?'

'You see, Winnie had an idea. It's a little off the wall, but I talked to the kids and they jumped at it. She wants to house-swap.'

'House-swap?'

'Yeah. We get the farm…she gets a manageable house in a beautiful street with wonderful neighbours.'

Molly couldn't help but laugh. The idea was so ridiculous that it almost made sense. 'Are you serious? This is what she wants?'

'It was all her idea. Obviously, there are things

to sort out. I'd have to get my roof looked at before handing it over to her. We'd have to figure out the kids' schools. But that's all doable.'

Molly gazed into Ethan's eyes. 'This is what you want to do?'

'Yes.'

'It's a pretty big risk.'

Ethan nodded and brushed a hand through her hair, tucking her curls behind one ear. 'You're worth it.'

Chills ran through her body from where he touched her. 'Why do I love this idea?' asked Molly.

Ethan's smile lit up his face. 'You think you might want to join us?' he asked shyly. 'After Romania?'

'Who needs Romania?' She'd been zigzagging the globe for the past six years. She knew now that it wasn't the travelling part of her life that filled her with passion; it was the part where she got to help people and animals. And she could do that here. She'd finally found somewhere she wanted to settle and people she wanted to settle with.

'Seriously?' asked Ethan.

'Seriously. I'm done searching for adventure. You guys give me plenty of excitement right here.' Molly suddenly thought of something.

'Won't you miss living so close to all your aunts and uncles?'

'Aunty Anne's already informed me that if we move, they're all coming to stay for Christmas, birthdays and any other holiday you can think of. And this place is so big we won't even be on top of each other.'

'But what about work?'

'We can fly in.'

'You trust me, after the storm?'

'Even more after the storm.'

Molly flung her arms around Ethan's neck, holding him as close as she could. He wrapped his arms tightly around her back and pressed her to him. She gasped when she realised something. 'I could start my animal sanctuary here!'

'Exactly. It's perfect.'

'You're perfect.'

He shrugged. 'I'm not bad.' Ethan pulled away and cupped her face with both hands. He stroked her cheek gently with his thumb. 'I'm so glad you found your way back to me. I think I've always loved you, and I know I always will. You're perfect with Maisie and the twins, and my whole family loves you as much as I do.'

Molly smiled happily. 'You're the family I've always dreamed of having. And the man I never thought I'd get. I certainly took the long way round, but I got here in the end.'

EPILOGUE

MOLLY SHUT THE door of her farmhouse and walked past the redbrick stables. She patted the heads of her donkeys as she passed and let the horses sniff her hands. She wandered onto the grass and eventually found Ethan, sitting under a tree near the marker for Heather's grave.

All wrapped up in a soft wool sweater and a cosy scarf, she held her mug with both hands and sipped her steaming coffee. It was late summer and today was the first day Molly had felt that autumn chill in the air. It was warm in the sun, but chilly as she passed under the shade of each tree.

'Is this seat taken?' she asked and joined him on the grass when he laughed.

The infamous pet-hating vet was currently scratching the head of a chocolate Labrador ex-police dog, and unable to get up because two of their three barn cats were snuggled up on his legs.

Molly smiled to herself and passed him her

coffee. Aunty Anne was still smug about finding them the police dog, and when Molly had finally met him she'd burst out laughing because he looked exactly like Ethan. Long, dark eyelashes and deep brown eyes. It was meant to be. He was a good-natured dream of a dog. He let the cats walk all over him—literally—and they were often found sleeping together in a warm pile on the kitchen tiles by the fireplace.

Kai, Harry and Maisie were all in the far horse paddock. They'd all decided to learn to ride since they'd made the move out here to the farm, and Kai had picked it up immediately. Now he was helping teach the other two. Harry was still an inch shorter than Kai, but he was getting there slowly. The twins sat on the fence and watched Maisie, still learning to mount a horse. They shouted encouragement at her, and she finally made it up onto the saddle. Molly and Ethan could hear her laughing all the way from their vantage point.

They'd been taking in injured and unwanted animals for a few months now, and Winnie's old farm was getting fuller every week. Retired service dogs, misfit cows and donkeys from farms that would otherwise be put down. They'd even found a lame emu for Harry, but they hadn't gotten him yet. He was going to be part of Harry and Kai's birthday surprise.

236 ONE-NIGHT REUNION WITH THE VET

They'd fixed the roof tiles and the chimney right after the storm, rebuilt the stables. Then fixed the roof in Ethan's old house for Winnie. She fitted right in with the old crowd on Ethan's street, and made the best barbecue chicken Ethan had ever tasted for the street parties. Winnie had even let them keep the lamb. They'd called him Joan Jett, never feeling the need to explain when people asked them why he had a girl's name.

Molly had liked her little green house, but she'd never really fallen in love with it. Not like this place. Here she already felt protective of every brick, every flower bed and every tree on the site. And her favourite people from the street, she'd brought with her. And the others, all the collected aunts, uncles and cousins, had visited them numerous times already. There was no shortage of company. The extended family was planning to spend the whole summer there, followed by Christmas, and Molly couldn't be happier.

Molly watched their third barn cat jump off the fence onto their still rather overweight British Saddleback pig. She walked in circles on its back before lying down for a snooze. The pig completely ignored her and carried on snuffling the ground and eating the grass.

Ethan took her hand and squeezed it. 'I'm so glad we found our way back to each other.'

Molly smiled and met his eyes, honey-brown

in the sunlight. 'I'm glad I finally found what I never knew I was looking for.'

'I'll have to think about that one, but I'm sure it was a compliment.'

Molly laughed and kissed him.

Ethan wasn't risk-averse anymore. He loved that Molly was a daredevil—after all, if she hadn't been willing to risk her life she might not have saved his sister. Some things were worth a risk. He saw now that Molly's adventurousness, far from being a negative, was actually a positive. He loved every piece of her.

Ethan was finally happy. Molly filled in all the gaps in his life.

And Molly finally had incontrovertible proof that she was loveable—a whole family's worth of it. Ethan made her feel special every day.

Surrounded by family and animals, neither of them would ever get the chance to feel lonely again.

* * * * *

If you enjoyed this story, check out this other great read from Zoey Gomez

The Single Dad's Secret

Available now!